#5

Winter Carnival

THE MITCHELL BROTHERS SERIES

#5

Winter Carnival

THE MITCHELL BROTHERS SERIES

Brian McFarlane

Fenn Publishing Company Ltd.
Bolton, Canada

WINTER CARNIVAL
BOOK FIVE IN THE MITCHELL BROTHERS SERIES
A Fenn Publishing Book

Fenn Publishing Company Ltd.
Bolton, Ontario, Canada

Distributed in Canada by H. B. Fenn and Company Ltd.
Bolton, Ontario, Canada, L7E 1W2
www.hbfenn.com

Library and Archives Canada Cataloguing in Publication

McFarlane, Brian, 1931-
        Winter carnival / Brian McFarlane.

(Mitchell Brothers series; 5)
For ages 8-12.
ISBN 1-55168-247-8

        I. Title. II. Series: McFarlane, Brian, 1931- Mitchell
Brothers series; 5.

    PS8575.F37W55 2004   jC813'.54   C2004-904389-7

WINTER CARNIVAL

Brian McFarlane, with 53 books to his credit, is one of Canada's most prolific authors of hockey books. He comes by his writing honestly, for he is the son of Leslie McFarlane, a.k.a. Franklin W. Dixon, author of the first 21 books in the Hardy Boys series. With his father in mind and with two brothers not unlike the Hardy Boys as his central characters, Brian has created a new fiction series for young readers—the Mitchell Brothers.

NOTE FROM THE AUTHOR

The Mitchell Brothers are on their way to visit their Uncle Jake in the North Country town of Storm Valley. They plan on enjoying the week long Winter Carnival and hope to cheer their favourite uncle to victory in the Carnival's premier event—the sled dog race. But a railroad disaster almost ends their journey before it begins. And a heart attack suffered by their Uncle Jake shortly after their arrival results in a major shift in plans. Max, a novice at sled dog racing, replaces his uncle in the race and relies on his Siberian husky Big Fella to play a major role and help him find his way. Then there are the trouble-making Bummer brothers who connive to make it almost impossible for the Mitchell brothers or the residents of Storm Valley to compete successfully in any of the Winter Carnival events. But if you've followed the previous adventures of Max and Marty, you'll know they are not easily discouraged or intimidated, even if it means trading blows with the bullying Bummers.

I had great fun writing this book. It's one of my favourites in the Mitchell Brothers series.

Brian McFarlane

CHAPTER 1

OFF THE RAILS

"What the…"

The Mitchell brothers were fast asleep when the gently rocking train jumped the tracks. They were jolted from their seats and knocked roughly to the floor. The railroad car jerked sideways. There was a horrifying screeching of metal on metal as the car pitched drunkenly on its side.

"Marty!" shouted Max. "You okay?"

The car rocked heavily. Passengers who moments earlier had been chatting or laughing, playing cards or reading books, had been flung in all directions like confetti. Some were piled atop others like football players in a scrum.

Marty rubbed his head. "I…I think so."

Marty guessed he had been knocked out briefly when his head hit the back of the seat in front of him. The Hardy Boys book he'd been reading had gone flying. That was all he could remember. It was a bitterly cold night, in 1936, and the brothers were on what was scheduled to be a two-hour journey from their home in Indian River to Storm Valley, where they planned to visit their Uncle Jake.

All Marty had been talking about for the previous two weeks was how much fun they were going to have at the Storm Valley Winter Carnival. His constant chatter was driving his older brother Max crazy. But suddenly a Winter Carnival was the last thing on their minds.

Max peered cautiously out the window. The train listed precariously and Max's worst fear was that the car would buckle and plunge hundreds of feet over a cliff onto the rocks below.

Gusts of swirling snow swept in through the shattered windows. Heavy suitcases that had been stowed in overhead racks had tumbled down, crushing several passengers.

"We have to stay calm!" Max shouted to Marty. "Don't panic!" Marty was still rubbing his sore head.

"What do we do?" he asked groggily.

Women were screaming and children were howling piteously. A few men shouted incoherently. The many injured lay moaning under the debris of tumbled luggage and broken glass. One frightened old man held his hand to his chest and was waving feebly for help.

"We have to get help!" Max said.

It was late afternoon and getting dark. Outside, flurries of snow and freezing rain sent a frightening chill through the car. The electric lights inside the car blinked out and somewhere among the tangle of bodies a mother moaned softly.

"Help me, please. Somebody help me. I've lost my baby..."

Marty Mitchell found himself being pulled to his feet by his older brother Max. He brushed pieces of glass from his red hair. "Max, what happened?" he stammered.

"Train wreck," said Max. "And it's serious. We're all lucky to be alive. You hit your head on the seat in front of you. Knocked you out for a few seconds. You okay now?"

"I guess so," Marty mumbled, feeling the lump on his forehead. "It's just a little bump." He looked out one of the broken windows. "Looks like we're on the edge of a cliff."

"Too close to the edge," said Max. "We almost went over the embankment and into the river. It's getting dark and we'll soon be freezing in here. We've got to move. Here's your book. It was on the floor."

Marty dusted off the book. "I wonder what the Hardy Boys would do in a situation like this?" he said wryly.

"Probably die of fright," Max answered. "Now put

the book away. I'll find our backpacks. There are flashlights inside. And I'll try to find our mitts and parkas in all this mess."

"What about Big Fella?" Marty asked. "He's with the other dogs in the baggage car ahead."

"We'll go find him," Max answered.

Max rummaged into his sack for a flashlight. He handed a second one to Marty. Max tossed Marty his parka and hurriedly slipped into his own. "The mitts are in the pockets," he said. "Let's go." He pointed toward the front of the car. "This way."

The brothers climbed cautiously forward, helping passengers to their feet, urging the able-bodied to assist others, and urging everyone to bundle up. Max heard a faint cry. He saw a tiny body in a pink parka wedged under a fallen duffel bag. He saw a baby's bright smile.

He hauled the duffel bag aside and picked up the infant. "Here's your baby, ma'am!" he shouted. "All safe and sound." The boys helped the hysterical mother to her feet. She was clutching her coat and they helped her into it.

"Your baby seems pretty fair, considering," Max reassured her. Through her tears she smiled gratefully. She mentioned something about going to meet her husband in Storm Valley. Marty found a blanket and helped the mother wrap it around the baby.

"Thank you," she said. "Thank you."

"Don't panic, folks!" Max scrambled through the car and tried to calm the passengers. He shouted, "If you are able, try to regain your seats, cover up and stay calm. Looks like the train left the tracks but this car is still upright. That's the good news. Is there a doctor aboard?"

From the darkness came a reassuring voice. "I'm a doctor." The man waved his arm and then climbed stiffly to his feet. He struggled to pull an overcoat free from some brown boxes.

"You okay, doc?" asked Max.

"Just shaken up, like everybody else." The man slipped into his coat. Max noticed that he appeared to be unsteady on his feet. Max hoped the doctor's head would clear. Several passengers appeared to be badly shaken up. They needed his help.

"Doc," said Max. "Take this flashlight and check for injuries. Any broken bones or concussions, well, you'll know what to do."

Next Max addressed the passengers. "Anybody who's hurt, call for the doctor. Meanwhile, my brother and I will try to make our way forward. We'll try to find out what happened. Nobody leave the car. It's freezing outside and snowing hard. Bundle up as best you can. There are extra blankets on the overhead rack. Someone find something to cover the broken windows. Cardboard from some of those broken boxes might do the job. Find some tape to

5

hold the cardboard in place. Stay close together to keep warm. And above all, try not to panic!"

Max felt a hand at his elbow. An attractive woman was just emerging from under a tumble of spilled suitcases and coats. "I'm a nurse. I'll help. And I have my niece with me. She can give me a hand." The nurse quickly regained her composure and began administering first aid to the crash victims. "Thanks," Max said. "We'll go ahead then."

Max and Marty stumbled forward until they reached the end of the car. When Max reached for the door handle he turned to Marty and said, "There's just one car—a baggage car—between us and the engine and its tender. "Remember we saw a lot of sled dogs being loaded aboard in Indian River. Be careful. Some of the huskies may be out of their cages, running around loose. We don't want to be attacked by a pack of frightened dogs when we go on through."

Marty nodded, directing the beam of his flashlight on the door handle. The dogs were bound for the big sled dog race in Storm Valley. The race was the highlight of the annual Winter Carnival festivities. "I just hope they're all right, especially Big Fella," Marty said.

Marty heaved open the door and a gust of wind knocked him back a step.

"Man, it's cold," hollered Max.

He noticed immediately that the baggage car had separated from the train. The connection had been broken in the derailment and the car was listing on its side along the tracks and partially over the embankment. The brothers slipped down the side steps to the rails and ran along them to the baggage car. They clambered up the steps and hauled open the heavy door. "Watch it!" said Marty. They fought to keep their balance on the icy steps.

When the accident occurred, the train had been heading up an incline along the side of a small mountain. Fortunately, the engineer had reduced the train's speed to a minimum. At any greater speed, a derailment would have sent the entire train hurtling over the side of the mountain and down into the roiling rapids of the Cariboo River hundreds of feet below.

"Listen!" said Marty. The darkened car exploded with the racket of barking dogs. Most of the boxes and cages had slipped and tumbled over onto their sides.

"Big Fella!" called Marty. "You okay, boy? Big Fella!"

Max grabbed Marty's arm. "Did you see that?" he asked.

"See what?" Marty answered.

"I thought I saw somebody slip through the door at the far end of the baggage car," Max said. "But I can't be sure. Just shadows, I guess. C'mon. Let's find Big Fella."

"It really stinks in here," Marty said, pinching his nose. Upturned sleds and racing gear blocked their path. Boxes of mail and provisions destined for Storm Valley littered the floor.

"Who are you?" a voice roared. Max and Marty froze.

Two men with flashlights stomped into the car and yanked the door shut. Mushers, sled dog drivers, thought Max. He'd seen them come aboard at Indian River. One of them tried to push the boys aside, "Them's our sled dogs."

"No harm meant, mister," said Max, who stood his ground. At seventeen, he was just as tall and in much better shape than the man who pushed him. "We were just trying to find our own dog, Big Fella."

The man apologized. "Sorry, boys. Must be the wreck shook up my good sense. I know you meant no harm. Just a man becomes awful attached to his dogs."

"We know," Marty said.

"What do you say you let Whitey and me handle this? We'll settle the dogs down and look after the ones that need care. You boys go on ahead. Find out what happened from the engineer."

"Good idea," said Max. "But we have to find Big Fella first. Where are you, Big Fella? Where are you, boy?"

There was a familiar yelp from the far corner of the car. Max and Marty hurried to find Big Fella hunched upright inside a tumbled box. The big Siberian husky looked a bit shaken, but was apparently safe and sound.

"Marty, look him over quickly," said Max. "We've got to keep going."

"He's fine," said Marty. "Nothing broken. He's awfully happy to see us."

Big Fella shook his head and barked.

"You can let him out now, Marty. He can come with us."

No sooner was Big Fella released from his box than his body stiffened, his lip curled and he snarled. Something lunged out of the shadows behind the Mitchell brothers. Then disappeared.

Marty swung round and grabbed Max by the arm. "Looks like a bear!" warned Marty. "Run for it!"

The bear loomed from the shadows. Big Fella, snarling and barking, crouched down, ready to attack. The bear roared defiantly and shook his huge head, flashing large yellow teeth. But Big Fella refused to back off, his own sharp teeth bared, his willingness to fight quite apparent. "Atta boy," encouraged Marty. It would take a more ferocious bear than this old bruin to make Big Fella turn and run! The bear sensed it too. Growling and shaking his head in annoyance, he slowly backed down and shuffled off to a far corner of the car. The other dogs, meanwhile, snarled and barked at the bear but wisely kept their distance.

Marty let go of his brother's arm. "I can't believe there's a bear on the train," he whispered. "How did he get in here? Who would allow such a thing? He scared the wits out of me!"

"Never mind that now," Max replied. "We've got to keep moving."

CHAPTER 2

TO THE RESCUE

Max didn't want to alarm his brother but he was worried that the baggage car they were standing in might lose traction at any moment and topple into the river. If so, he wanted Big Fella to have the same chance he and Marty had—a chance to jump to safety.

While Big Fella nuzzled their legs and feet, Max and Marty pulled the door open at the far end of the baggage car. A blast of snow and wind almost hurled them back inside. The engine and its coal-carrying tender, separated from the rest of the train, were just ahead. The Mitchell brothers gasped. Engine and tender were clear off the rails. The engine, hissing steam, was tilted at a dangerous angle and its cow-catcher protruded over the lip of the steep ravine.

Max and Marty saw movement atop the tender. Two men—the engineer and the fireman—were sprawled on top of the coal car, looking dazed and confused. Both men were bleeding from cuts on their heads.

Max shouted into the wind, "Hey, there! You men better jump and do it now! That old engine may slide over the cliff at any second."

"Can't jump!" the engineer shouted back. "We're hurt bad. Broken bones in our feet, we think."

"Hold on!" Marty called out.

The boys dropped into the snow and waded through the waist-high drifts to the engine. Big Fella was right at their heels.

"Boulder on the tracks," the engineer explained as the Mitchell boys climbed closer. "Couldn't stop in time. Didn't see it until it was too late." He groaned and wiped blood from his cheek.

"Never mind that now. We've got to get you down from there," Max urged. "You're in real danger."

The engineer chuckled grimly. "You're right about that." He could see the jagged rocks of the river far below. "We'll climb down from the tender. There's a ladder..."

The boys crawled through the drifts to the ladder. The huge engine suddenly lurched and slipped a few feet farther over the edge.

"Holy smokes!" blurted Marty. "They may not make it. It's going to be close." Smoke billowed from the engine's stack, steam hissed from its sides. The men tried to hurry even though they were crawling over slippery chunks of coal, fuel for the red-hot furnace they'd just abandoned, its glowing coals of no value now.

The two railway men were in a life-and-death struggle to get to safety. And they were crawling quickly despite their injuries.

Max reached up and helped one man gingerly, easing him down the ladder and into a bank of snow. The man's left foot was twisted awkwardly.

"Thanks, kid," the man grunted.

"Now let's get your partner, the fireman," said Marty.

The boys were helping the second man down the ladder when the engine lurched and began to inch sideways—toward the brink of the cliff. Marty shouted, "Hang on!" It shuddered and stopped. Max began to lose his footing. Big Fella leaped forward, and using his strong teeth, grabbed Max by his leather boot. The husky pulled hard, holding Max back, helping him to regain his balance.

"C'mon. Hurry!" shouted Max.

"She's going over!" Marty screamed.

"Let go of the ladder!" Max screamed at the fireman. The big man obeyed and dropped face first into the snow, bringing Max down with him. The fireman howled—first in pain, then in relief. Had he refused to give up his grip on the ladder, he would have perished. Horrified, they watched the engine begin to slide sideways again, its big wheels sawing through ice, snow and mountain rock. Then it toppled over the edge. It tumbled end over end until it smashed into the rapids of the Cariboo River. There was a flash of flame and a burst of steam.

But the crisis wasn't over.

"Help me!" shouted the fireman, waving his arms. His body had begun to slide, following the icy track made by the heavy engine.

"Oh, no!" shouted Max, reaching out to grab the man's pant leg.

The fireman cried out. He tried to brake himself with his hands. But the slope was steep. He realized he was sliding toward the edge of the cliff. And pulling Max with him!

"Max, let go of him!" shouted Marty. No one would have blamed Max if he'd relaxed his grip on the man's legs and saved himself.

"No way!" he shouted back. "We can save him." He looked over his shoulder. "Hang onto us, Big Fella! Don't let go!" The husky dug all four paws into the snow and tightened his grip on Max's boot. Marty rushed over and reached out to grab the other foot. Marty quickly hooked his own boots over the nearest iron rail of the track. "Pull, Big Fella!" he shouted. "Hang on, Max! We've got you!" Marty's arm muscles quivered. They were as tight as piano wires. But pulling together, he and the big husky were able to haul Max and the fireman away from the brink. Soon they were safe on flat ground. They lay between the rails, gasping for breath. But safe for now.

"You all right, mister?" Marty asked. The man shook his head. "Thanks to you and your brother."

"And one heckuva strong dog," Marty said, giving Big Fella a hug.

The fireman pulled himself up on his elbows. He wiped snow and ice from his grimy face. "I was almost a goner," he said in astonishment. "You boys saved my life. You and your husky." Big Fella leaned close and licked the fireman's face.

"You did good," said the engineer. "Now I'm counting on you to save my passengers."

Max and Marty hurried back to the baggage car and spoke with the two mushers and some other men who gathered to help. "We've got to get the engineer and the fireman to a hospital," Max explained. "And there's a man aboard who may have had a heart attack. There's a small hospital in Storm Valley. Can you rig up your sleds and take the three of them there? It's not far. I figure it's only a couple of miles to town."

"I think so," said one of the mushers. "Our sleds are in okay shape. Looks like someone took an axe to a couple of our sleds. Don't ask me why. All our dogs are in fair shape. Yeah, we can do it. But it'll take us awhile to get set up." He looked down at Big Fella. "Say, that's one fine looking husky you've got there. Care to sell him?"

"Not a chance!" Marty answered. "Not a chance in a million."

"If you'll take care of the injured, we'll go on ahead," Max said. "Most people were just shaken up. More frightened than hurt. We should reach town ahead of you. We'll get someone to come back for the rest of the passengers. I just hope there's another engine and some railroad cars in Storm Valley. Rescuers can't come back by car. The road is slick with ice and covered with snow."

"Go ahead, then, boys. And good luck to you," one of the mushers shouted into the wind. A second musher, impressed with the way the blond-haired youth was handling the situation, called out, "Say, how old are you, kid?"

"I'm seventeen," Max answered. "My brother's fifteen."

The Mitchell brothers grabbed their packs. They pulled the hoods of their parkas tightly over their heads and started out along the tracks, leaning into the strong wind. Big Fella led the way, nipping at the snowflakes, delighted to be involved in such a grand adventure.

Not far up the tracks they came across the boulder that had derailed the train.

"Wow! It's a huge one," Max said. He pushed at the rock with his boot. The rock didn't budge.

"No wonder the engineer couldn't see it in time to stop," Marty said. "Not in this weather. The rock must have broken off from that rocky ledge up there and rolled down the hill onto the tracks."

"Wait a minute, Marty," Max said, grabbing his brother by the arm. "Look over there! What's Big Fella up to?"

The husky was sniffing and pawing at the snow. Then he darted up the incline, sniffing and whining. He turned to look at the brothers and barked several times. "Looks like he's sniffing out some other dog smells," Max said.

Curious, Max scrambled up the incline and came upon a place sheltered from the snow and wind by a growth of small evergreens.

"Marty! Big Fella's found something up here."

Marty watched his brother. He disappeared but emerged a few minutes later. He scrambled back down the incline. "Somebody's been up there," he explained. "And not too long ago. There's an old shed up there, next to a frozen pond."

"You find anything else?" Marty asked.

"Footprints in the snow, for one thing. And some sled tracks. But look at this. Here's a chocolate bar wrapper. It's from a Hershey bar. And a couple of cigarette butts. Sweet Caps."

"What do you think it means?" asked Marty.

"Hard to say," Max said, frowning. "But I think it means someone brought a dog sled out here and waited in the shed for the train to come up the grade."

Marty gasped. "You mean this wasn't an accident?"

Max shook his head. "Someone deliberately rolled that big rock down the hill and onto the tracks. Someone wanted the train to crash."

"But why?" asked Marty.

Max carefully put the wrapper and cigarette butts into the pocket of his jacket. "I don't know, Marty. But we sure want to find out, don't we?"

He broke into a jog, running between the rails and Marty followed, hurrying to keep up, Big Fella at his side. "Hey, Big Fella, if you weren't such a smart dog, Max would never have found those clues," Marty said.

Big Fella barked.

"And who'd have thought our week long visit to Uncle Jake's would start out with a monster train wreck?"

CHAPTER 3
UNCLE JAKE'S PLACE

It was Monday morning. Somewhere outside Uncle Jake's house, a rooster, blinking into the dawn, crowed loudly. The wind was still brisk but it was no longer fierce. Snow had drifted high along two sides of the barn and the driveway would require some energetic shovelling.

In the warm kitchen of his log home, Uncle Jake, a tall, handsome man in his mid-forties, handed his nephews steaming cups of hot chocolate to go with the big meal of bacon and eggs and toasted sourdough bread they were wolfing down. Big Fella, having already emptied his bowl and having been out for a run, stopping only to attend to some personal business in the woods, slept on the well-worn rug next to the hot wood stove, a bowl half-filled with water next to him.

"I called your folks first thing this morning," Uncle Jake said as he buttered another piece of toast and smothered it with strawberry jam. "Woke them up and told them the news. They were relieved to know you both came through the train wreck in fine shape. Your dad, being in the newspaper business, said he'd write a story about the accident for tomorrow's paper. Said he'd mention how you two pulled the railway men to safety and then sought help. Said you had to promise not to let the free publicity go to your heads."

"If Dad wants some good quotes, I can give him some," Marty said, grinning. "I'll tell him that I was a big hero rescuing everybody in sight while Max was being scared half to death by a mangy old bear."

Max rewarded Marty with a trace of a smile and then bit into his buttered toast.

"Any news from the Chief?" asked Marty.

"Nothing yet," said Uncle Jake. "He sure surprised me when he came pounding on my front door in the middle of the night."

Hours earlier, Uncle Jake had been jolted awake by the thump, thump, thump of Police Chief Connolly's big fist against his door. He was stunned when he threw it open and saw his nephews, along with their husky, shivering on his front porch. Chief Connolly's patrol car was idling in the driveway.

"Their train didn't make it but they did," the Chief had said, nodding at the Mitchell brothers. "And quite the young heroes they are, far as I can tell."

"Come in, lads, come in," Uncle Jake had said, stepping back. "You too, Chief. Tell me about it. What's happened?"

Uncle Jake had ushered them in and helped the boys off with their parkas. He had listened, wide-eyed, while Chief Connolly told him about the train derailment and how his nephews had probably saved a couple of lives. And how they had hurried into town seeking help for the other passengers. "The boys can tell you the rest," he said. "If they're not too tired. They're great lads to have done what they did. Showed a lot of courage and grit." Then he had hurried off. "Got lots of things to do before morning, Jake," he had called over his shoulder. "I've got to see to those passengers when they get to town. Make sure nobody froze to death."

Now, over breakfast, Uncle Jake wanted to hear more.

"So you slogged through the snow into town and went right to the police station?" asked Jake.

"That's right," said Max. "Luckily, Chief Connolly was still on duty. He'd been called in to investigate a break-in at the hardware store. He said he called you earlier and told you not to bother meeting the train, that it was behind schedule because of the storm and might not arrive until this morning."

"Yes, he did call. And I asked him to call me back when he learned something more. Then I fell asleep,

I guess, sitting in my rocking chair by the fire."

"We told Chief Connolly we thought someone deliberately tried to derail the train," Marty said, eager to talk. "But I don't think he believed us. He said to us in that raspy voice of his, 'You boys must be kidding me. Why would anyone do that? There was nothing of much value aboard.' I told him my Mom thinks I'm pretty valuable. He laughed at that. Anyway, he called the hospital and was told that two mushers had just brought the injured railway men in on their sleds. And the man we thought had a heart attack was fine. Just scared to death, I guess."

"Either that or he had indigestion," said Max. "Then the Chief called the head man at the Railroad Company..."

"That would be Charlie Foster," Uncle Jake interrupted, his head now buried in his icebox. "I know there's more milk in here somewhere," he muttered. He emerged smiling, brandishing a bottle. "And what did Charlie say?"

"Mr. Foster said he'd get right on it. Said he'd round up a crew and get the other train engine in town fired up right away. Said he'd hook a couple of old passenger cars to it, fill them with blankets and stuff and get right to the scene of the accident. Then the rescue train would back up into town. They should be here by now."

"Later, Mr. Foster will send a crew back with some

heavy equipment to get the cars from the derailed train back on the tracks," Max added. "He wants to clear the line as fast as he can so that people can get here for Winter Carnival."

"But the old engine that was pulling our train is a goner. It's rusting at the bottom of the Cariboo River," Marty chuckled. "It dropped from the cliff like a bomb—a real fish-squasher. Splat!"

Uncle Jake blew softly across the top of the mug.

"I feel badly for those folks on the train," he said. "I'll bet a lot of them were on their way here for Winter Carnival. The opening ceremonies take place at noon today."

"We're going, aren't we?" Marty asked.

"Course we're going," said Uncle Jake. "There'll be band music and hot dogs and free popcorn and oh, yes, lots of pretty girls. And the Mayor will make one of his famous long-winded speeches. If they had a prize at the Carnival for the biggest windbag, he'd win it hands down."

Uncle Jake looked at his watch, rose from the table and threw on a plaid jacket.

"You boys finish your breakfast. I'll go feed my dogs. Be back in a minute."

When he was gone, Marty turned to Max. "How come Uncle Jake never married?" he asked. "Mom says he was engaged once—to the best-looking, smartest girl in Storm Valley. But her mother didn't like Jake. How could anyone not like Uncle Jake?"

"That was a long time ago," said Max. "Remember, Jake was a lumberjack and a prospector when he was young. And he played pro hockey for a while—with Vancouver when they won the Stanley Cup in 1915. Back then some mothers didn't want their daughters dating hockey players. Or lumberjacks or prospectors, either."

"I get it," said Marty. "Those men were always away. Never home when you needed them. Always in danger of getting hurt. Those mothers wanted their girls to marry doctors and lawyers—men others looked up to. "

"Pretty much, I guess. Anyway, Uncle Jake joined the Army and was wounded in France in the Great War. He was missing in action for a long time. I guess the girl got tired of waiting for him to come back."

"Or her mother talked her into marrying someone else," said Marty.

"I think that's what happened, although Uncle Jake never talks about it—except to Dad. Dad told Uncle Jake once that he should consider moving to Florida, that it's a good place to mend a broken heart and marry a rich widow."

Marty snickered. "Sounds like Dad. The rich widow part, I mean. And what did Uncle Jake say?"

"Dad said Uncle Jake laughed and told him, 'Rich

widows wouldn't be interested in an old North Country bumpkin like me. You can't raise huskies in Florida. And what rich widow would want to come live in Storm Valley? In a drafty log house with a bunch of dogs underfoot all day?' "

"This house isn't drafty. It's a great house," said Marty.

"Do you remember the time Uncle Jake showed up at our house in Indian River with a cute little puppy?" asked Max. He chuckled. "That was at Christmas four years ago. He told us the one he gave us was the pick of his litter. That was Big Fella."

"He was right, too," said Marty. "I remember he pulled a photo out of his wallet. It was a photo of Balto, Big Fella's great grandfather, a beautiful grey and white Siberian husky. And I blurted out, 'I hope this puppy turns out to be a big fella like him.' Mom said that was the perfect name for the puppy."

"Uncle Jake told us that Balto was a hero," Max said. "He once led a dog team from one town to another in Alaska—six hundred and fifty miles—to deliver some kind of serum that stopped an epidemic and saved a lot of lives. Balto was on the trail for over five days with little food and water."

"And in subzero temperatures," Marty added.

The boys heard footsteps on the back porch.

"Here comes Uncle Jake," said Marty. "I'll pour him another cup of coffee."

CHAPTER 4
LOOKING FOR A LEAD DOG

"We should let him out, Uncle Jake."

Max passed the sugar bowl across the table and nodded toward Big Fella. "He'd love to run with your dogs."

"Give him a few more minutes," said Uncle Jake. "After all the excitement of last night's train wreck, he needs his rest." Uncle Jake chuckled. "Besides, I have some things to say and Big Fella might like to hear them."

He tilted his chair back and linked his hands behind his head, "Boys, I never thought when I invited my favourite nephews to Storm Valley for Winter Carnival week they'd get involved in so much excitement right off the bat. Good thing you two weren't badly injured."

Max took a sip of hot chocolate. "I suppose it's amazing we weren't all killed. Most of the other passengers were just shaken up. One lady was a little panicked. She lost her baby in all the confusion but we found it for her. And a nice nurse came along to help her out."

"I guess you could call it a miracle," agreed Uncle Jake, coming down off the heels of his chair. "I hope the Chief can figure out who caused the wreck."

He sipped at his coffee and looked down at the sleeping husky. "Boys, tell me about Big Fella," he said. "Appears to me that you're raising him well. He looks to be in pretty good shape."

"He's in great shape, Uncle Jake," Marty said. "You taught us all we know about dogs, especially Siberian huskies. You told us when you brought him to us that he'd have a tremendous desire to run. You were right about that. Big Fella runs everywhere. He's the fastest dog in Indian River. We hook him to a sled on wheels and he loves to pull that around. He gives rides to the kids in town.

Marty gave Big Fella a friendly cuff behind the ear.

"And you told us to make sure he had other dogs to run with. He's got lots of dog friends at home. He runs with the neighbour's dogs—a Dalmatian and a pair of setters—all the time. And Max and I run in the woods with them—almost every day."

"Does your Mom still get mad when Big Fella digs holes in your backyard?"

"Mom just pretends to get mad," chuckled Marty. "She says he digs faster and deeper than the local gravedigger," Marty said, chuckling. "Some of the holes he digs look like craters on the moon. Dad says his ancestors must have lived near the Grand Canyon."

"Well, I warned you and your folks about that," said Uncle Jake. "And I warned them that Big Fella would shed his thick coat once a year. By now, your Mom has probably seen more fur than Goldilocks."

"Yep. Sometimes our house looks like one big furball." Marty said. "We're bringing him up proper. We even built him a nice house with a flat roof. He likes to sleep on the roof—just like you said he would."

"Don't get me wrong, Marty," Uncle Jake said, leaning back in his chair again. "I'm not checking up on you. Just curious. How strong do you figger he is?"

"Strong? Big Fella? He's as strong as Atlas," Marty bragged. "Why, half a dozen of us kids piled on a long toboggan last week and Big Fella pulled us all over town. We'd ride down the hill and he'd pull us right back up. I say that's mighty strong, wouldn't you? Why, if he'd been leashed to that train engine last night he would have pulled it back from the cliff and planted it right back on the tracks."

Max sighed, shaking his head. "If he did that we'd be calling him an elephant, not a dog. But why so much interest in Big Fella? You know how strong and fast he is. He's worked with your sled dogs often enough the past couple of seasons—every time we come to visit. I think maybe you're getting at something."

Uncle Jake grinned at his nephews. "I am getting at something," he admitted. "There's a good reason I asked you to bring Big Fella with you this week. You know I always enter a team in the sled dog derby at Winter Carnival time. I'm proud to say I've won it twice. But my last win was five years ago. My lead dog, Randy, is fourteen and can't run any more. Arthritis has slowed him down. Shoot," he said, rubbing his knee. "Slowed me down, too. I thought of retiring from sled dog racing and then I thought of Big Fella. Maybe he could lead my pack. Maybe, even though he lacks experience, he could help me win the derby one more time. The winner gets five hundred dollars."

"Wow!" said Marty. "That's worth shooting for."

Max looked down at the sleeping dog. "But doesn't it take a lot of racing experience to become a good lead dog?" he asked.

"Well, yes, it does. But Big Fella is exceptionally smart. He's had some experience and he catches on fast. We have a few days this week to work with him. Race isn't until Saturday. I've already put in my entry fee but I could always pull out if Big Fella isn't up to it."

"Isn't up to it!" exclaimed Marty. "Uncle Jake, I think it's a great idea! I'd love to see Big Fella lead your team to victory. What do you say, Max? Wouldn't that be neat?"

"It would be more than neat. It would be fabulous," Max answered. "I've often wondered how Big Fella would do in competition. I never dreamed you'd want him as your lead dog for the main event—the sled dog derby. I thought…"

"Say it, Max. You thought what?"

"Well, Dad suggested that I enter him in the weight pulling competition for dogs at the Winter Carnival. But maybe he'd do better, and have more fun, in the derby."

"Hey, he could do both," Marty said, leaping to his feet. "He could be a two-time champion. He frowned. "Max, what is a weight pull…whatever you called it?"

"Let me explain," said Uncle Jake. "The dog sled is positioned at a start line and the sled is loaded with weights. Just one dog pulls as much weight as he can. When the whistle sounds, he has one minute to pull the sled twenty-five feet to the finish line. Last year's winner was Coalfoot. That dog, believe it or not, pulled two thousand pounds."

"Wow!" Marty said, eyes wide in surprise. "I didn't think any dog was strong enough to do that. A horse maybe. Or an elephant."

"I'm not sure Big Fella could pull that much weight," frowned Max.

"He could try," Marty said, excitedly. "What we'll do is hold up a big steak at the finish line. That would really inspire him."

"Uh, uh," laughed Uncle Jake. "No steaks. No fish. No incentives of any kind allowed. The handler can't even touch his dog. Hand signals and verbal commands only."

"That's okay," Marty said. "I still think Big Fella can win. Let's go for it." He had another thought. "Is there any prize money involved in that event, Uncle Jake?"

"There sure is. A hundred dollars to the winner."

"A hundred bucks! That's for us," Marty exclaimed.

"It would be nice to go home with some cash in our pockets," Max agreed.

"And our pictures in the papers," added Marty. "Say, maybe there are some other events we can win. Go home with a million bucks and loaded down with gold medals. Won't the kids at school be jealous?"

"Now don't get carried away, Marty," grinned Uncle Jake. "But there are always lots of events at the Winter Carnival. There's the fishing derby, the skating races on the lake, the curling events at the arena and the ice sculpture competition. The lumberjacks will compete in pole climbing and log sawing and arm wrestling." He grimaced and shook his head.

"There's a new event this year, a bear wrestling contest."

"Bear wrestling!" said Marty. "But that's crazy. Who would be fool enough to wrestle a bear?"

Uncle Jake nodded and raised a finger. "I can think of some fools who would. The Bummer brothers."

"I know the Bummer brothers from hockey," Max said. "They're big and they're tough, with heads as hard as curling stones."

"It's not just that bear wrestling is a foolish event. I think it's cruel to the bears," said Uncle Jake.

"They wear muzzles, don't they?" Marty asked.

"Who?" asked Uncle Jake. "The bears or the Bummer brothers."

"The bears, I mean, not the Bummers..." Marty said, before realizing Uncle Jake was pulling his leg. "Oh, you're a funny man, Uncle Jake."

"Maybe they should put muzzles on the Bummer brothers, too," added Uncle Jake. "They're a mouthy lot, and always spoiling for a fight. They get that from their dad, Bart Bummer."

"I know they break all the rules in hockey," Max said. "Indian River beat the pants off Storm Valley in the playoffs last season. Three of the Bummers were on the local team and they were troublemakers. Always fighting and taking penalties. A bunch of sore losers."

"Yeah," Marty said. "Max scored three goals against them and they tried to put him out of the game with some dirty play. Then they piled into the referee and all three of the Bummers got suspended. Look up Bummer in the dictionary and you get 'Bad News.'"

Max shook his head at the memory. "They were about the dirtiest hockey players I've ever seen."

Marty turned to his brother. "What about you, Max? Care to wrestle a bear this week? Pick him up over your head and toss him out of the ring?"

"I'll pass on bear wrestling," he said. "But I may take a crack at the skating races."

"You should, Max. You're the best hockey player in Indian River. And the fastest skater."

"I should warn you," said Uncle Jake. "This race is more like a free-for-all—because of the Bummer brothers. It's a two-mile event—a mile to the end of the lake, a turn around an oil drum there, and then back again. There are always about fifty skaters entered, including the five Bummer boys—three of them fast, two of them slow. The fast ones try to win; the slow ones try to keep anybody else from winning. It gets rough out there on the ice, so if you enter, better wear some elbow pads."

"First things first," said Max, getting up from his chair. "Uncle Jake, if we're going to get you ready for the sled dog race next Saturday, we'd better find out if Big Fella still remembers what to do. Why not hitch the dogs up and go for a spin through the woods?"

"I was just going to suggest that," said Uncle Jake, reaching for his big parka, his gloves and his plaid scarf.

As though he'd been listening, waiting for those very words, Big Fella jumped to his feet. He looked excitedly at Max and Marty as if to say, "Come on, guys. Isn't it time for a little exercise? I'm ready for a run."

CHAPTER 5

THE BUMMERS CONSPIRE

Across town in a shanty by the lake, Bart Bummer, foreman of the local lumber mill, called his five sons together for a meeting. The young men ranged in age from seventeen to twenty-three and they were a surly, insolent lot. They were all school dropouts, smokers, drinkers and all-round troublemakers. They dressed in hand-me-down clothing and rarely shaved or bathed. Losers all. Except for one thing: they were all champion farters. Gleefully breaking wind at any time and at all times—even at the dinner table. Storm Valley's priest, Father Costello, had once confided in Doc Green. "I'm actually glad they're not Catholic. But if they were Catholic and came to mass—we'd have people lighting candles all over the church. I'm afraid the church would explode."

No wonder folks in Storm Valley gave the Bummer boys a wide berth whenever they saw them coming. The truth was, wherever the brothers gathered trouble was bound to follow. Halloween was their favourite day of the year. There were outhouses to topple and rotten apples to throw at little kids out trick or treating. The only kids who knocked on the Bummer front door on Halloween did it on a dare. Or they were new kids in town. When Bart Bummer opened the door, dressed like the devil and brandishing a flaming three-pronged spear, kids ran screaming up the street. The rest of the Bummers, if they weren't out burning scarecrows or stealing candy from younger kids, would laugh uproariously at their father's shenanigans. Almost everyone in town drew a sigh of relief when Halloween was over.

The Bummers couldn't be trusted. Uncle Jake once said, "I'd rather shake hands with a porcupine than have any dealings with the Bummers. Be sure you count your fingers after putting your paw in theirs."

For some reason their given names all began with the letter B. There was Bert, twenty-three; Boris, twenty-one; Billy, twenty; Brutus, eighteen; and Babe, seventeen. Brutus, the husky eighteen-year-old, was nicknamed "Bad Boy" or "Bully" because of his reputation for delinquent behaviour and because of his constant attempts to intimidate younger, weaker boys in town. Babe, named after his father's favourite ball player, Babe Ruth, was a carbon copy of Brutus, almost as muscular and just as mean-spirited. "He's probably the smartest guy in the poolroom," was about the highest praise anyone ever gave Babe.

Bart Bummer was proud of his offspring. "Chips off the old block, they are," he'd brag to what few friends he had in town. "When my wife Mildred ran off years ago, after telling folks all those lies about how I mistreated her, I brought the boys up myself. She tried to get 'em away from me but I put a stop to that. I can't tell you how. But you can be sure I brought them up my way. No hugs and kisses, no sappy birthday parties or Christmas treats. I brought them up to be hard men in a hard world. They don't take sass from nobody, 'cept from me, of course." He'd slap his knee and cackle.

He'd laugh and say outrageous things about other townspeople. Behind their backs or to their faces, it made no difference to Bart. He wasn't a big man but he had fists like rocks. While he slurped black coffee from a cup at the Bo Peep restaurant, he'd pour Heinz ketchup over his grilled cheese sandwich and fries while other diners nearby would nervously try to ignore his loud, obnoxious opinions and his dreadfully cruel jokes. They'd all had run-ins of one kind or another with Bart—or his sons. These incidents brought back memories that were never pleasant.

The good people of Storm River tried hard to tolerate the Bummers. But if lightning had struck the

Bummer shanty, setting everything ablaze or if a sudden flood had washed their pitiful shack away, with all six hanging to the roof beating their breasts and screaming for help, their neighbours might have become temporarily blind or turned deaf as fence posts. More important matters might have kept them from rushing to the scene and attempting a rescue.

Bart spent most of his evenings drinking at the local tavern—the Muddy Mug. The weary bartender would serve the mean-spirited old foreman and then move away. He'd take a cloth and dry a few glasses or wipe an imaginary spot off the far end of the bar. He'd reminisce angrily about the time the Bummer brothers trashed his place—almost ruined it—all because he'd refused to serve a pitcher of beer to two Bummer sons—then teenagers. The bartender had threatened to call Chief Connolly. "Then do it," Bart said. His eyes became small black bullets. "Just remember this: I might get an urge to burn your building down some night—with you in it. On your tombstone we'll write: Here Lies the Barbecued Bartender." Bart chuckled at his own joke and was pleased to see the bartender's face turn chalk white. Bart promised to pay for all damages, of course. But he never had. Besides, he knew Chief Connolly would never investigate any charges. He was a squeamish man when it came to the Bummers, never sure how he'd fare if it came down to a confrontation with them.

The bartender recalled a time when a newcomer to town, while attempting to join in a casual conversation with the mill foreman, had asked Bart how many of his sons were married.

"Married!" he'd roared. "None of them are married. They're too mean to marry. What sane woman would have any one of 'em? And that suits me to a T. Marriage almost ruined me. No reason for it to ruin them. End of story."

Bart had turned his broad back on the newcomer while the other men in the room had squirmed in their chairs. Especially the married ones. The newcomer had gulped down his drink and slipped out of the bar, shaking his head, bewildered by what he'd heard.

"Winter Carnival's here again, boys," Bart Bummer was saying. His sons were grouped around the kitchen table drinking mugs of strong coffee. Bert, the eldest, carelessly hurled a log into the fireplace, sending sparks flying. A few more burn marks in the faded carpet wasn't going to bother anybody, Bert moodily thought. But if a few flying embers set one of his brothers' clothes on fire, he grinned, that might rouse his dad's attention. Bert promised himself to take better aim with the next log.

Bart Bummer frowned at Bert, then continued, "You boys listen good. As foreman of the mill, I'm giving you all a few days off to get ready for the week's events. You all work for me and I told old Mr. Chips, the mill owner, we were taking a little holiday during Winter Carnival. Told him if he didn't like it he could lump it. What's he gonna do? Fire me? Fire all of us? Well, he won't do that, will he? Unless he wants to find his new car in the lake someday—with him at the wheel. So forget him. He's a spineless old fart, anyway."

His boys grinned. Pop always looked out for them. He talked tough, he acted tough, and he was tough. Brutus laughed out loud. He had a vision of old Chips sitting in his car, sinking to the bottom of the lake. Then his hat rising to the surface. Lots of bubbles. Then his cheap toupee bobbing on the surface, next to his hat. "Ha, ha, ha," he roared while the others stared at him curiously.

"See this thumb," Bart said, raising his fist, his big thumb sticking straight up. He was enjoying his role of entertainer. "Well, maybe you can't see old man Chips, but I can. He's right there under my thumb. And that's where I plan to keep him."

This time all of his boys roared with laughter. They knew their dad had coerced Mr. Chips into making him foreman. Pop was so funny. Babe said, "I can see him, Pop. Old man Chips is trembling and about to go in his pants. Press your thumb on the

40

table and you'll squash him. So long, Mr. Mill Owner. Goodbye, Mr. Chips."

There was another burst of laughter.

"We won't squash him—not just yet—but we'll squash anybody else who gets in our way," Bart Bummer growled, all humour gone now.

"Listen, boys. Pay attention! About the Carnival. I've imported four new dogs from a breeder in Minnesota—real beauties they are—so I should win the big race on Saturday. Babe, you can drive my second team. I should win the five hundred dollar first prize money and you better grab second place money of two hundred and fifty dollars—or else."

"Who's your toughest competitor, Pop?" Boris asked.

Bart Bummer smiled slyly. "Well, two real good mushers—fellows named Whitey Carson and Busher LeBrun—were headed in from Indian River on last night's train." He stopped to chuckle, his mean little eyes full of mirth once again. "I reckon Babe and Brutus here may have fixed it so those two and all their equipment are headed back to where they came from. I say, good riddance! So my main competitors are out of the picture and out of the race. Isn't that right, Brutus?"

Brutus swallowed hard. "Well, not exactly, Pop. You see..." Fearful of his father's wrath, Brutus fell silent.

"Spit it out, you jackass!" roared the father, pounding the table with a big fist. "What do you mean, not exactly?"

Brutus burst out blubbering.

"Pop, the plan backfired. The train went off the tracks and instead of the folks on the train going back to Indian River like we figgered they would, the railroad sent a spare engine and a couple of cars from Storm Valley to pick everybody up and bring them back here."

"You mean to say the two mushers are here in town—in Storm Valley?"

"Yeah, Pop. Carson and LeBrun and all their dogs are here in Storm Valley. They were shaken up but they arrived in pretty good shape and they say they'll be ready to compete."

"What about their sleds? I hope you took good care of their sleds."

"We tried to, Pop. I swear! As soon as the train went off the rails we jumped aboard the baggage car. Nobody saw us and we found the sleds and started breaking them apart with a hatchet. But then..." Brutus turned to Babe, looking for support.

Babe said, "We just got started when we were chased out of there by a bear, Dad. Honest. A full-grown bear came running at us. Scared us half to death. We had to run for our lives."

Their father banged his fist on the table a second

time. "You two nincompoops! You're telling me there was a bear loose on the train. In the baggage car with all those dogs in there. I think there must have been a bull in there, too! Because your story is all bull."

"No, Dad, we saw a bear," Babe insisted. "Honest!"

"Honest? We don't hear that word often in this house."

He slapped the table again, hard. "See what happens when you send a couple of boys to do a man's job!" Bart growled like a bear and his boys nodded obediently. "These two couldn't just stop the train. They had to knock it off the tracks. They couldn't just sneak into the baggage car in all the confusion and bust up a couple of sleds. A bear chased them off. It must have been a grizzly bear to scare the pants off you stumblebums—if there really was a bear."

"Far as we could tell it was a brown bear," said Babe.

"But it could have been a grizzly," added Brutus. He turned to his older brothers. "Yeah, in fact, I'm pretty sure it was a grizzly. Wouldn't you guys run from a grizzly?"

Bert and Boris just laughed. "Sure we would," teased Bert. "If it was a grizzly. And if there were any grizzlies within a thousand miles of here. And if the grizzly bought a ticket and took a train to get here.

Let's face it. You scaredy-cats were chased by a dog."

Boris said with mock innocence, "Maybe it was a mean old teddy bear that scared you half to death. They can be ferocious. I heard of a case where one hugged its owner to pieces. Honest."

Babe and Brutus stood there, their cheeks aflame with anger and embarrassment.

"Aw, lay off of them," scowled Bart Bummer. "We got bigger fish to fry."

He pounded the table a third time. "Dang! I didn't figure on the railway having a spare engine in town. But no matter. If their sleds were damaged and their dogs were spooked, Carson and Lebrun will be in trouble. They won't have a chance to run the course more than once. So they'll be at a big disadvantage. You boys got anything else to report? You didn't run into a panda bear, by any chance?"

"No, sir," mumbled Babe. "But it wasn't our fault. We thought the train was going to slow down to a crawl on the incline. And it did. We thought it would stop short of the rock and cause some confusion. But with the snow and all, the engineer didn't see the rock and he hit it harder than anybody figured. We ran into the baggage car but everything in there was a mess. And it was dark in there. We managed to do some damage to the sleds like you asked us to...but then this bear came at us..."

Bart Bummer clapped his hands together. "There's

that dern bear again! Taking a little train ride around the north. Chasing my boys around a baggage car. Can you believe these two? Are you sure you didn't see three bears? And where was Goldilocks while all this was happening? And don't tell me she was taking a bleepin' nap."

"Well," continued a rattled Babe, "forget the bear. A couple of young guys from Indian River came along—Jake Mitchell's nephews—remember them—the hockey players? We had to get out of there fast—before they spotted us. We ran and hid in that little shed in the woods—the one all the kids used as a change house when we used to go swimming in the pond. Through the cracks in the boards we saw the engine slide over the cliff. We didn't mean for that to happen. And we saw the Mitchell kids and their dog rescue the engineer and the fireman. Those kids were pretty brave, you ask me. Those railway men were hurt bad. They almost went over the cliff with the engine…"

"Yeah, Pop, we almost became murderers," Brutus said.

"Baah! Don't even mention that word," glared their father. "It was an accident, pure and simple, a common rock fall caused that wreck." He waved a finger at each of them. "And don't you boys forget it."

"There's something else, Pop," Brutus said. "The

Mitchell kids had a husky with them. I heard them call it 'Big Fella.' We figured Jake Mitchell might borrow the husky to replace his lead dog in the big race."

Bart Bummer laughed. "Jake Mitchell hasn't won a derby race in five years. His dogs are almost as old as he is. A new lead dog isn't going to make any difference. Forget about old Jake. He's about done as a sled dog driver. Done like dinner. When the going gets rough, he'll quit like a broken watch."

"What about some of the other events?" asked Boris, impatiently. He was anxious to get back to a card game being held down at the poolroom.

"I'm getting' to them," said the father. "Boris, you're the fastest skater in the family, aren't you? Then you better win the race." He glared at the others. "All of you will take part. It's a mile up the lake, around an oil drum and back again. Boris will win the prize money and we'll share. If anybody gives Boris a challenge, the rest of you take care of him. You know what I mean. Make him wish he'd stuck to roller skating or ballroom dancing."

Boris said, "This Mitchell kid you were just talking about—the older one—is a great hockey player back in Indian River. He's mighty fast on his skates—I mean really fast. I've seen him go."

"Then knock him off his feet. That'll make him really slow. And remember, boys, always make things look accidental. The judges won't dare disqualify any of us."

"Yeah, why is that, Pop?"

"Because we're Bummers, bird brain. You kiddin'? They're all scared to death of us. Intimidation gives you power to do what you want. It always gives you an edge..."

"There's good prize money for the best ice sculpture and the fishing derby," Billy piped up. To this point he'd remained silent. "And I guess a couple of us will be in the pie-eating contest. Then there's a new event—bear wrestling."

"Bear wrestling?" sputtered Bart Bummer. "Bear wrestling?" He glared at his sons. "Why didn't some-one tell me there was bear wrestling?"

"It was a last-minute decision," Billy said. "The bear's owner was in Indian River this week. He called and said he'd come here for a fee and the organizers of the carnival said, 'Come on up.'"

Bart glared at Babe and Brutus. "Don't you two git it?"

"Get what, Pop?" They said in unison, looking bewildered.

"What a pair!" said Bart. "I'd knock your heads together but all I'd get is sawdust all over my nice clean floor. That bear you saw on the train. It was coming here for the bear-wrestling contest. And it made you run like a pair of rabbits. Why, that bear was probably the tamest bear you'll ever see. And you thought it was a man-eating grizzly. Well, you can all get ready to meet him again because one or two of you are going to be wrestling that bear."

He turned back to Billy and said, "We surely will be in the pie-eating contest. It only costs a buck to enter, doesn't it? Forget about ice sculpture."

"But Pop," said Babe. He was hopeful of sculpting something on his own, perhaps a mother bear with her cub. Last year his stupid brothers had sculpted a sled dog doing its business in the snow. His brothers had thought it was funny. So did some of the loafers at the poolroom. But the women in town had called it disgusting.

"You hard of hearin', boy? I said forget about it! No more wastin' time on a sissy event. That's final!"

"Yeah, Pop," sighed Babe. "I hear ya."

Bart pointed a finger at the group. "One more thing. Jake Mitchell won the ice sculpture last year with a moose. We don't want him winnin' it again. You hear me? Do what you have to do."

The Bummer boys nodded. They got the message.

"Then that's it, boys. Meeting's over. Get off your butts and get to work." He rose from the table and slapped Bert on the back. "Boys, we should clear a few hundred bucks easy at the Carnival this year. That'll pay for a big family party when it's over."

CHAPTER 6

UNCLE JAKE SUFFERS
A SETBACK

The harness was old and heavily patched, but it would have to do. Max Mitchell went over it inch by inch, testing every strap and buckle. He'd spent practically every minute with Uncle Jake learning about sled dog racing techniques. There was so much to know.

"I'm teaching you all I know about the sport," Uncle Jake had said to Max earlier in the day, "because you said someday you may want to become a driver."

It was Tuesday afternoon and Marty looked at the racing sled sceptically. "What do you think of this old thing?" he asked Max.

Max was hopeful but cautious. "I think it's fine. Old but strong. Uncle Jake made the sled himself. It's in good shape."

"But is it good enough to win the big race on Saturday?" Marty asked.

"Who knows?" said Max. "Anything can happen in a sled dog race. And Big Fella has never been tested as a lead dog. What do I know? I'm just a beginner. As green as a shamrock."

Marty grinned and offered a suggestion. "Maybe when you get to be a hotshot driver like Uncle Jake, I should sit in the sled and point you in the right direction. Case you get lost. You know I've got the eyes of an eagle. In the book I'm reading, *The Tower Treasure*, the Hardy Boys always stick together—like brothers should."

Max laughed. "Marty, I read that book. As I recall, Frank Hardy's kid brother Joe was smart enough to listen to his older brother and obey his every command."

"Go on. He did not."

"Joe Hardy was a very mature young man," Max continued, keeping a straight face. "He knew his older brother was someone to look up to, someone he should never question and always obey. That's why Frank liked him so much. In our case, well..." Max waggled his fingers and sighed.

"Get outta here," Marty scoffed. "That's so much bull. You can't con me," Marty responded. "I know you think I'm a great brother. If you don't think so, then I'll go across town and join the Bummer brothers. They'd love to adopt me as a brother, I bet. Then you'd be sorry."

Max laughed out loud, thinking of Marty mingling with the Bummers.

"You'd be right at home there," he said. "I hear they're all good farters."

Marty frowned. He punched his brother on the arm. "Speaking of the Bummers," he said, "do you think they might have caused the train wreck?"

"Hmm, not likely," said Max. "They may be troublemakers but they're not murderers. And whoever rolled that boulder onto the tracks must have known someone could have been killed."

"Then who could have done it? Must have been someone from Storm Valley."

"Right. Could have been a disgruntled miner or prospector. Someone with a grudge against the railroad. Uncle Jake says there's a crazy old hermit who lives in the woods near the railroad tracks. The Chief arrested him once for throwing stones at the train. He was angry because it made too much noise. Could have been him."

Marty shrugged. "I don't think so. It would take more than one person to dislodge that rock," he said. "I wish the Chief would spend more time on the investigation. Seems to me he wishes we'd never told him we thought it was deliberate."

"Well, he's understaffed," said Max, "and hasn't much time it being Winter Carnival and all. But let's get back to the subject of you coming with me in a sled dog race—if I ever get to drive in one. The less weight on a dogsled the better. That's why you can't sit up front. And I won't get lost, Marty, I promise. There are markers all along the trail."

"But if I sit up front," Marty persisted, smiling slyly, "and you come in first, I'll be the real winner 'cause I'll be sitting just ahead of you at the finish line. But, hey, I'll share the prize money with you, Max. You know, like a good brother should."

Max stifled another laugh and circled the sled. He threw Marty into a headlock. "Hey! Ouch!" laughed Marty.

Max whispered in his brother's ear. "I said passengers aren't allowed. There are rules against it. And if they were allowed you'd weigh down the sled so much I'd never get to the finish line."

Marty pulled away, pretending to pout. "Okay. But I can help you get ready for your racing career. I can be your coach and manager and trainer all in one."

Max gave in. "Okay, you can call yourself coach, manager and trainer if you want," he said. "Call yourself the head dogcatcher for all I care. But this isn't hockey or baseball. Sled dog racers don't have coaches, managers or trainers."

"Then I'll be the first one," Marty grinned. "Now let's get the dogs and hook 'em up."

"Okay. While you get Big Fella and the other dogs,

I'll give this rig a final check. Uncle Jake will be out in a minute."

Max bent over to peer under the sled and Marty couldn't resist. He punched some snow together in his mitts and hurled the missile at his brother, striking him on the backside. Then he turned and ran toward the dog pen, laughing and shouting over his shoulder, "Remember I'm your coach. You've got to show me some respect."

Max said, "Yeah, sure," as he quickly rolled a ball of snow and, taking careful aim, tossed it at his fleeing brother. In summer, Max was a pitcher of some renown. He had a great arm and his snowball struck Marty squarely on the back of the neck. The force of the blow sent Marty sprawling. He landed headfirst in a snowbank and emerged wiping snow from his eyes, his nose, his ears and his mouth. He giggled and raised his hands over his head. "You win. No more snowballs. I surrender."

"You better," Max shouted, turning back to the sled.

A moment later, a snowball crashed into his shoulder. When he turned, he saw Marty disappearing behind the barn, his laughter ringing in the cold winter air.

A few minutes later Marty was back with the dogs, bounding through the snow. All of them were anxious to be fitted to the harness, sensing the fun and excitement of a run through the woods.

Big Fella, too, whined with anticipation.

"Gosh, you'd think he knew there was a big race coming up," said Marty, rubbing the husky between the ears.

"Smartest dog I've ever seen," Max said. "If there's a smarter dog or a braver one in all of the North Country, I've yet to meet him."

"He was smart enough to sniff out those footprints in the snow after the train wreck," Marty said, "and find that cabin by the pond. We may never know who was sneaking around there."

"I'll bet Chief Connolly writes if off as an accident," said Max. "The footprints and sled marks we told him about have been covered over by now. And when I offered to turn over the chocolate bar wrapper and cigarette butts as evidence, he wasn't interested. Just shrugged and said, 'Heck, anyone could have left them there.' Hey, here comes Uncle Jake. Dressed like a musher. Looks like we're going for a ride."

"You're going. You're the lucky one," sighed Marty. "I get to stay home."

"Your turn will come," said Max.

"That's right," agreed Uncle Jake. "Marty, we'll go for a run first thing tomorrow. Today, I want to test Big Fella as my new lead dog."

Big Fella barked, as if he knew he was being discussed.

The husky enjoyed the frigid temperatures, the company of the other dogs, the excitement of the run, and the sheer joy of following the trail. He was elated to be what he was—a sled dog in winter.

Uncle Jake gathered his other dogs together, getting them ready for the harness. He laughed and fed them biscuits as they danced around him, yipping with excitement. They sniffed curiously at Big Fella, and he returned the sniffing ritual, greeting them affectionately, happy to be back among friends.

Even though several inches of snow would cushion the feet of the dogs as they romped along the trail, Uncle Jake brought along a number of custom-made leather booties to protect his dogs' feet if they ran into rocky or icy terrain.

"You hop in the sled and pull that blanket over you," Uncle Jake told Max. "We'll go for an easy spin. Along the way I'll give you a few more tips about sled dog driving."

Max put one foot in the sled and then turned to Marty. "You might want to shovel off the driveway while we're gone," he needled. "You know, build up your muscles."

"Sure, Max, I'll do that," Marty answered. "Get him out of here, Uncle Jake, before he comes up with any more bright ideas."

"Let's go, Big Fella! Hike!"

The husky lunged forward, the other dogs following obediently. "Looks like they've already accepted

Big Fella as their new leader!" Uncle Jake shouted. "My father told me something about sled dogs years ago and I never forgot it."

"What was that, Uncle Jake?" asked Max.

"He said, 'Unless you're the lead dog, your view never changes.'"

He became serious. He explained to Max that "Hike" is used to start the team moving; "Ahead" means do not turn; "Gee" means to turn right; and "Haw" means to turn left. "Of course, 'Whoa' means to stop," he added.

"You taught Big Fella and me all those commands last year," Max reminded his uncle.

Uncle Jake remembered. "But it never hurts to go over what you know. 'Basket,'" he continued, "is where the mushers stow their gear. Or where an injured dog is loaded. The 'hand bow' is a curved piece of wood or handle that helps balance and steer the sled."

"You taught me a lot about a sled dog's diet, Uncle Jake. You said water is the most important thing."

"Right. Good, clean water. And they don't get water by eating snow. That saps a sled dog's energy. A bowl of warm water after a drive in cold weather is to a sled dog what a hot chocolate would be to you and Marty—a nice treat."

"And you told me fatty foods provide the dogs with quick energy."

"Fats and protein and carbohydrates—all are important in a sled dog's diet. I figger 32 per cent protein, 15 per cent carbohydrates and 53 per cent fat."

They zigzagged through a trail in the woods. "Big Fella is a born leader, a natural," Uncle Jake said enthusiastically. "And I think you have the potential to be a great driver, Max. A good musher is like a good jockey on a fast horse. He knows when to hold his team back and when to let it go."

Uncle Jake might have also likened a good driver to a good hockey player—one who instinctively knows what to do on the ice. And Max was certainly a good hockey player.

Jake envied his brother Harry, having sons like Max and Marty. He thought of his own lonely existence, and how a wife and a couple of sons or daughters would have enriched his life.

"But Emily Ashmore, the love of my life, married Harvey Hillman, the funeral director, when I was away at war," he muttered. "And I never met another gal like her."

"Did you say something, Uncle Jake?" Max called out.

"Well, I was thinking we should organize a game of shinny while you're up here," Uncle Jake responded. Every time the brothers visited in winter, Jake would plow off a nearby pond and round up some of the neighbours for a hockey game that would last for hours. The war wound he'd suffered—a bullet through the leg—never seemed to bother him when he skated. And with his long strides he could still outskate men half his age. But he could no longer keep up with Max who was one of the best skaters he'd ever seen.

"Keep skating like that, nephew, and the NHL clubs will soon come calling," he told Max one day. His praise was as genuine as his pride.

He recalled Marty asking in mock annoyance, "Hey, what about me? Don't you see a lot of Vezina in me, Uncle Jake?" Marty was referring to Georges Vezina, the former Montreal Canadiens' goaltender after whom a trophy had been named.

"Uncle Jake sees a lot of hot dog in you," Max had quipped before Uncle Jake could answer. And they'd all laughed.

At the end of the day, all the players would gather in Jake's kitchen for hot chocolate and brownies. The latter Jake had baked himself.

Years went by and Jake told himself he didn't really mind living alone. There was a trout stream nearby and Jake fished it regularly. His small garden flourished each summer. He played chess with a widower down the road and sang in the church choir. He dabbled in oil painting and a man from the city once drove a hundred miles to see them. He bought six and told Jake, "You should charge more. You've got an eye for colour."

Jake recalled the day he heard that Emily Ashmore had left her husband. The funeral director had kept a drinking problem a dark secret for years. Kept his bottles hidden in coffins. But one day he fell down drunk and toppled into a coffin—right on top of old Miss Crouch who'd just passed away. A cleaning lady had witnessed the fall and was scandalized. She told everyone in town including Emily. When Emily reproached her husband he'd struck her in anger. Emily moved out of town the very next day and started divorce proceedings.

"I wonder where you are now, my Emily," Jake muttered.

"What did you say, Uncle Jake?" Max asked. "Did you suggest a game of shinny? That would be great. Let's try to work it in."

"We'll do that, Max," Jake shouted. "Although it's going to be a busy week."

After they'd travelled a mile or two, he pulled out a stopwatch. "We're already a minute or two ahead of the pace my team set last week when Randy was my lead dog. That's pretty fast."

"I love to hear the dogs breathing hard and their paws hitting the ground," said Max.

The team had crested a hill when Uncle Jake, who'd been loping behind with long, easy strides, felt himself getting winded. Suddenly, he applied the brake and brought the sled to a halt. He staggered a few paces from the sled and leaned heavily against a tree. He said, "You take over, Max, I'll rest awhile." The dogs looked back curiously. They were just getting warmed up and the sudden stop surprised them.

It surprised Max too. He jumped out of the sled and took his uncle by the arm. "You okay, Uncle Jake?"

"I...I guess so," Uncle Jake replied putting a hand to his chest. "Feel a little dizzy, is all. And I have a bit of a pain in my chest..."

"Here. Take my arm," Max said, somewhat alarmed. He helped his uncle into the sled and covered him with the blanket. "I think we better get you to the hospital."

Uncle Jake didn't answer. His eyes were closed and his breathing was ragged. Max knew he'd better hurry.

"Hike! Big Fella! Hike!" Max hollered and the sled surged forward. If Max was nervous about guiding the racing dogs through a narrow trail in the woods, he didn't show it. He kept a tight grip on the hand bow and guided the sled smoothly along the narrow trail. On one long downhill stretch he rode on the runners. *This would be great fun*, he said to himself, *if I wasn't so worried about Uncle Jake.*

He guided the sled through a thick stand of evergreens and over an embankment. Below was the main road leading into town. Max steered the sled through an opening and had to work hard to keep it from toppling on its side when it skidded onto the hard-packed surface.

"Gee!" he yelled, and Big Fella responded, turning right, turning toward the town's small hospital.

"Let it out, Big Fella, Hike! Hike! Hike!" urged Max. The dogs fairly flew over the hard-packed snow and barrelled straight down Main Street. On the sidewalks, people were gathered in small groups. They gawked when the sled raced along the snow-covered street, the dogs straining, Max shouting for more speed.

At that moment, some distance ahead, two of the Bummer boys—Brutus and Babe—were leaving the poolroom. They neither saw nor heard Max approaching because they were arguing loudly as to which of them was the better pool player. One pushed the other and was pushed right back. The shoving match carried the boys off the sidewalk and into the street. Only then did Babe Bummer holler, "Look out!" as he and his brother stumbled right into the path of the onrushing team of huskies.

"Haw! Haw! Coming through! Make way," shouted Max, heaving to turn the sled and the dogs into the centre of the street to avoid a collision. Big

Fella's great strength saved the day. He literally hauled the sled to the left, just missing the Bummer brothers, who sprawled in the snow and slush.

There was no time for Max to stop and explain. Or even apologize. The sled raced on, bound for the hospital at the end of the street.

When the Bummer boys realized what had happened, their blood hit a boiling point.

Brutus growled angrily, "What dern fool would pull a stunt like that? That fool almost killed us."

Babe wiped slush from the back of his pants. "That was the Mitchell kid," he said.

"Oh, yeah? The kid was showing off," Brutus decided. "Somebody ought to teach him a lesson."

"I guess it's up to us to do it," Babe said, grinning meanly.

Brutus nodded. "That kid will wish he'd never heard of Storm Valley when we get through with him."

At the hospital, Max waited patiently for news. Finally, Dr. Green came out and told Max he'd better go home.

"Come back in the morning," the doctor said, putting an arm around Max's shoulder. "It looks like your uncle may have suffered a mild heart attack. We're going to keep him overnight for tests and observation. He's sleeping now."

On the way back up Main Street, driving the dogs at a moderate pace, Max worried about his uncle. *He won't be able to enter the sled dog derby now*, he thought. *Or make an ice sculpture. Or do much of anything*, he realized sadly. It's a good thing he and Marty were there to take care of the dogs. *We'll miss the Carnival*, he thought to himself. *Marty will be devastated. But Uncle Jake's health comes first*, he knew.

"Stop right there!"

Two hulking youths were blocking Max's path. The sun was setting behind them and they were in silhouette. He didn't recognize them but the voice behind the threat sounded familiar. They appeared very menacing. He ordered the dog team to stop and released the ice anchor. The heavy hook grabbed hold and the sled skidded to a halt.

The two youths moved aggressively toward him. Max recognized the pair as the youngest of the Bummer brothers, Brutus and Babe.

"Hey!" Max said in a friendly tone. "I'm really sorry about almost hitting you guys. I was rushing my uncle to the hospital and I'm no expert at driving a dog sled. But it was an emergency and..."

"You should be sorry, you worthless so-and-so," snarled Brutus Bummer. He was chewing on a Hershey bar. He crumpled up the wrapper and tossed it in Max's face.

"You'll be a lot sorrier in about two seconds,"

promised Babe Bummer. He roughly seized Max by the arm.

A crowd had congregated, forming a circle. Men spilled out of the tavern, most of them anxious to see a fight.

"Wait a minute," said Max. "My uncle had a heart attack. Don't you understand?" He pulled away, but not before both brothers piled into him, knocking him backwards. He fell heavily to the ground. The Bummers began flailing at his face and body with wild but stinging punches. Max covered up as best he could, and when his attackers tired momentarily, he leaped to his feet. He could feel blood gushing from his nose. With no choice but to fight back, he yanked down hard on the hood of Babe's parka. Then he threw a roundhouse punch that landed crisply on Babe's jaw. Babe howled in pain as the blow sent him spinning. Max tried but couldn't avoid two solid punches to the stomach thrown by Brutus.

"Ooof," grunted Max. He thought for a moment he would go to his knees. He staggered, but refused to go down. He jumped back, narrowly avoiding a wild uppercut from Brutus. He moved in with a solid left hand that caught Brutus in the gut. Brutus grunted painfully and kicked out with a booted foot. It missed.

Just then, Big Fella leaped into the fray, dragging

the other sled dogs with him. Brutus howled like a wounded wolf when Big Fella's sharp teeth sank deep into his leather boot. Brutus scrambled to free himself. But Big Fella struck again. This time his sharp teeth caught the seat of Brutus' pants.

Riiip!

His red suspenders snapped as Big Fella pulled back, holding the pants in a vice-like grip.

"Heeelp!" screamed the blubbering Brutus. The folks crowded in the circle erupted in laughter when Big Fella shook his powerful head and yanked the bully's pants down around his ankles. Another head-shake by Big Fella and Brutus was thrown off balance. He toppled onto his back, wheezing, his thick legs sticking up in the air and his red long johns on display for all to see.

The laughter from the onlookers was deafening.

Suddenly, all the fight and all the bullying had gone right out of the Bummers. Babe's face finally emerged from under his parka and he put a trembling hand to a cut lip. He used the same hand to wipe the tears from his eyes.

"You did that!" he whimpered at Max. As if there was some local law against hitting a Bummer. "Nobody hits me like that and gets away with it," he threatened.

"But I just did," Max said calmly. "Give me any more trouble, and I'll do it again."

Babe appealed to the crowd for sympathy. "Look at my poor brother," he said. "You saw that wild dog attack Brutus! And for no good reason!"

"Hey, Babe," an old man snickered. "I counted at least two good reasons and they both begin with the letter B." The man next to him drew a big laugh from the crowd when he wisecracked, "Folks, wouldn't it be a shame if that husky got rabies from biting a Bummer. Ha, ha, ha, ha!"

"He had a dern good reason to bite him," someone else piped up. "He was protecting his master—like a good dog should. It was two against one until the dog jumped in. You ask me that made it an even fight."

"Yeah, and for once the Bummers lost," said another man, speaking from the back row. "I'm glad I was here to see that." He called out to Max: "You and your dog did well, son. You showed us all a lot of grit."

During this exchange, Brutus Bummer was busy trying to regain some semblance of dignity. Two little boys circled round him, laughing at his red underwear. Brutus stepped out of what was left of his pants, and kicked the remains in the air while the crowd hooted. He shook off his parka and wrapped it around his waist.

"Come on, Babe. Let's get on home," he growled, skulking down the street. Then he turned and pointed a menacing finger at Max. "That...that wolf of yours better not have rabies," he snarled, "or you'll go to jail."

"He doesn't and I won't," Max replied. "It was sure nice meeting you boys. I guess we'll be seeing you again soon."

"Thash right. Uh, oo can bet the fahm on it," sneered Babe, through his heavily swollen lips.

CHAPTER 7
THE FISHING CONTEST

To the surprise but delight of the Mitchell brothers, their Uncle Jake was back from the hospital early the next morning. "Hospital's cold and crowded," Dr. Green explained. "Jake will do better at home. And I live just a couple of blocks away."

"We'll give him lots of tender, loving care. I'll do the cooking," Marty volunteered.

"Oh, no," groaned Max. "Cold soup and hot dogs."

Dr. Green brought Uncle Jake home in his fancy new Oldsmobile. "Wow! That's the kind of car I'm going to own someday," Marty said, walking all around the doctor's car. "And I'll travel all over sitting on the hood so I can wave to all the girls."

"Is that right?" asked Max, winking at Doctor Green and helping Uncle Jake out of the passenger seat. "And while you're sitting on the hood, with your behind roasting from the engine heat, who's going to be driving the car?"

"My chauffeur, of course," Marty fired back. "I may be the only player in the NHL with his own chauffeur. I'm going to be a goalie with the New York Rangers, Doctor Green."

Max sighed and shook his head. He turned to the doctor. "A couple of days ago, Doctor Green, Marty told Uncle Jake he planned to play shortstop for the New York Yankees. We all wish he'd make up his mind."

"Never mind Max, Doctor Green," Marty said, gently kicking one of the tires on the Olds. "He's just afraid I'll get to the big leagues before he does. The truth is, I'll probably play for the Rangers in the winter and the Yankees in the summer. After I get thirty or forty shutouts and about a hundred home runs I'll probably buy a Rolls Royce. By then I'll have a valet too and be married to some famous Broadway actress."

"Well, a Rolls Royce is certainly a step up on this Oldsmobile, isn't it, Jake?" said Doctor Green. He came around the car, took Uncle Jake by the elbow and guided him up the walk to the house. "Easy now, Jake," he cautioned his old friend.

To Marty he said, "When you wind up playing for the Yanks and the Rangers, Jake and I will come to New York and see you play."

"And we'll put that chauffeur to work," Uncle Jake said. "He can drive us all around Broadway. People will stop and point and say, 'There goes Marty

Mitchell's famous car with some VIPs in it.'"

"Uncle Jake, I'll have him drive you anywhere you want to go. You can stop in at the restaurant I'll own by then. All famous athletes own restaurants. Say, what are VIPs, anyway?"

"Very Important Persons," said Max as he opened the front door. "Say, here's an idea. Because the two seasons overlap, you can see Marty win the Stanley Cup one night and star for the Yankees in their home opener the following afternoon. And then, after that, you can watch him win the world heavyweight boxing championship and maybe bowl a couple of perfect games. If he's not too tired, you might get to see him jump off the Brooklyn Bridge. Or swim the Atlantic."

"And why not?" asked Marty huffily. "Although bowling perfect games may take a little practice, especially since I've never been bowling in my life."

"Sounds like you're going to be a champion at something, Marty," Doctor Green said, chuckling. "Why not start with a couple of first-place finishes in the Winter Carnival events?"

"You mean we're going to be able to take part in Winter Carnival after all?" asked Marty.

"Well, why not?" said Jake. "Takes more than a small heart attack to keep me from Winter Carnival."

"Great!" said Marty.

Then he said seriously, "Uncle Jake, we decided to stay close to you today. Tomorrow's going to be my big day. I figure I'll be a cinch to win both the pie-eating contest and the fishing derby."

"Doesn't take much athletic skill to win either of those two events," said Max. "Just sheer luck in the one and an empty stomach in the other—a big empty stomach."

"My stomach and I will work together like a well-oiled machine," Marty answered confidently. "We'll swallow those pies like the whale swallowed Noah."

"That's Jonah," corrected Max. "The whale swallowed Jonah."

"Whatever. As for luck at fishing, I've always been lucky at everything. The only bad luck I ever had was getting stuck with a brother who doubts I'll ever achieve any of my dreams."

"Not true," Max responded. "It's the bragging about them that gets me. And to prove I have faith in you, little brother, I'll give you ten dollars if you win either the fishing contest or the pie-eating contest tomorrow."

"Hey, that should be money in the bank for me," Marty replied happily. "Not meaning to brag, of course."

The boys helped their uncle into his rocking chair, which they had pulled close to the fireplace. From the closet, Marty brought a colourful Hudson Bay blanket and placed it over his lap.

"Jake gave us a bit of a scare," the doctor told the Mitchell brothers over hot tea in the kitchen. "But I took some tests and his ticker's still tickin' and I think he'll live a good many years yet. I gave him some pills to take. Just don't let him near a dog sled for the rest of the season. You boys will be leaving for home soon so I've arranged for a nurse to stop in every day. She's also agreed to do the cooking."

"Hurrah!" shouted Max.

Uncle Jake had been listening from the other room and called out, "She better be a good looking nurse, Doc. And one who likes dogs. Otherwise, no deal."

"Oh, she's good looking, all right," laughed the doctor. "She'll be here tomorrow morning. She's new in town and you'll be her first patient."

When the boys finished the chores in the house and in the barn, Max took the dogs for a long run. Marty insisted on making the meals that day—peanut butter and jam sandwiches for lunch and bowls of canned soup for dinner.

"Some cook," Max muttered, raising his spoon. "Is that all we get—soup?"

"I tried making scrambled eggs but the shells fell in. And then I burned them. Burned the toast, too. And the bacon. So I gave your dinner to the dogs.

They loved it. Here, have some bread."

Uncle Jake ate his soup without comment. Then he rested and read the Farmer's Almanac and a couple of joke books Dr. Green had given him. He chuckled over some of the contents. "Listen to this," he said, slapping his knee.

"This fellow owned a dog that was so dumb it suffered fourteen concussions—all from the toilet seat falling on its head."

Max chuckled but Marty groaned. He said, "I bet lots of kids wouldn't get that joke because they don't have indoor plumbing and toilet seats. They go to the outhouse."

"And here's another one. A fellow in California claims he's invented an insect that is more productive than any other insect. He crossed a honeybee with a lightning bug and now he has a bee that works all night."

This time both boys groaned.

Uncle Jake flipped a page and plunged on. "Oh, and here's another one. A little boy asked his grandfather, 'Granddad, can you make a noise like a frog?' The grandfather says, 'Sure I can. Why?' And the boy says, 'Well, Grandma says when you croak we're all going to see Niagara Falls.'"

Max and Marty burst out laughing. "That's a good one, Uncle Jake," Marty said.

"One more. A fellow's mother-in-law came to visit

and he tried to make her feel right at home. He said, 'Mom, my house is your house.' And she said, 'Great. Get the heck off my property.'"

The room filled with laughter.

"And then the mother-in-law said, 'Don't worry about me. I'm going out every morning and I'm going to jog ten miles a day—no matter what.' And the son-in-law said, 'She's been gone for ten days now and we don't know where the heck she is.'"

"That's enough, Uncle Jake," snorted Marty. "My sides are starting to hurt."

"And I've got to go to the bathroom," Uncle Jake stated. With help from the boys he rose from his chair. He insisted on walking down the hall on his own.

"Now look what you've done," Max said sternly.

"What?"

"It's your cooking. Uncle Jake probably has diarrhea."

Max turned and ran when Marty took a wild swing at him.

"Well, boys," Uncle Jake said, growing serious on his return, "I promised Dr. Green I'd take it easy for a spell. That means I'm withdrawing my team from the sled dog race. Too bad. I was hoping you boys would be here to see me win it."

"Not so fast," declared Max. "Your team is still in the race. But it has a new musher—me."

Uncle Jake shook his head. He laughed and slapped his hands together. "Max, that's great. You've got driving skill and stamina. Your big problem is lack of experience. A rookie driver has never won this race."

"Then it'll be a first, won't it? A first for both Big Fella and me. The race is a few days off. I'm sure there are still lots of tips you can give me before then. And you can do that from your rocking chair."

Uncle Jake rubbed his chin, thinking. Finally, he said, "Max, it's a crazy idea." Then he grinned. "So crazy, in fact, it just might work."

The next morning, Max and Marty woke up to the smell of bacon sizzling on the stove and hot coffee in the pot. Marty said, "I smell hot biscuits. Jake must be baking. And he promised to take things easy."

But when they entered the kitchen, ready to admonish Uncle Jake for making breakfast, a chore Marty was determined to do, Uncle Jake was sitting at the kitchen table, enjoying his first cup of coffee of the day. And he had a big grin on his face.

They knew immediately the reason for his happy look. At the stove a slim woman with curly blonde hair and wearing a white dress with an apron tied around her waist, flipped crisp strips of bacon out of a frying pan and onto a plate. She was about to crack eggs for frying when she heard Max and Marty enter the room. She too was wearing a happy face. Jake must have been telling her jokes from his joke book, Max thought. The woman stopped to give her hands a quick wash.

"You must be Max and Marty," she said, wiping her hands on a towel, "I'm Emily Ashmore. I'm an old friend of your uncle's. I'm going to be looking after him for a few days."

"But we know you," Max said, surprise on his face. "You're the lady we saw on the train. Remember us?"

"Of course, I remember you," Emily laughed as she shook Max's hand even more vigorously. "You and your brother were very heroic. I remember how quick you were to take charge. But I didn't know you were Jake Mitchell's nephews. How nice to see you again."

Marty looked confused. "But I thought Uncle Jake was getting a nurse to look after..."

"I am a nurse," Miss Ashmore replied. "Recently graduated and fully qualified." She gave Jake a fond look. "And hopefully capable of controlling an obstinate man like your uncle, who is already planning all kinds of mischief in the days ahead. I'll have my hands full with him, I'm sure you'll agree. I may need your help to keep him in line."

Marty laughed and sat down at the kitchen table. He reached for a piece of toast.

"It's very nice to meet you, Miss Ashmore. We'll

help you tie him down if he doesn't obey your orders. We can practice our Boy Scout knots on him."

"Please call me Emily, boys."

"I won't need any tying down," Uncle Jake growled over his coffee cup. "And if I did it would take more than you young pups to do it. Besides, I have good reason to be on my best behaviour with Emily."

"Why is that, Uncle Jake?" Marty asked.

Uncle Jake put his cup down and ran his fingers around the rim. "Boys, Emily and I go back to high school days here in Storm Valley. We were great friends growing up. Then I went off to play pro hockey and work in the bush. Then the war came along and we drifted apart. Some things happened in her personal life so she moved to the city some time ago to get her nursing degree. And look, now she's back. You can imagine how surprised I was when she walked in that door an hour ago. That rascal, Doc Green, knew I'd be shocked, too." Jake tapped his chest. "Wonder it didn't give me a real heart attack. That man must be looking for more patients."

Emily laughed and said, "Well, Jake, Doctor Green didn't tell me who my first patient would be, either. I was just as surprised as you were. Obviously he planned it that way." They both laughed and looked fondly at each other. Max and Marty grinned, exchanging looks. They sensed that Emily Ashmore was about to make quite a difference in Uncle Jake's life.

Emily turned to the boys. "Jake mentioned my personal life a moment ago. I was married years ago to a man everyone said was solid and reliable. But appearances can be deceiving and he turned out to have a violent temper. And a drinking problem. So I left him and then divorced him. Fortunately we had no children..."

"But you had a young girl with you on the train," Marty interrupted. "Wasn't that your daughter?"

"No, she's my niece," Emily explained. "My niece lost her parents in a car accident when she was very young and I'm raising her. She's a lovely young woman. We just rented an apartment a few blocks away. She's already caught up in the spirit of Winter Carnival. In fact, she's entered in one of the events this morning."

Max hurried through breakfast and then excused himself. "I want to spend a couple of hours on the trail," he explained, getting up from the table. He planned to spend as much time as possible guiding the sled. He realized with each outing he would become more confident, more at ease. He was aware the other mushers, men like Busher Lebrun and Whitey Carson would have their dogs in peak condition. They'd have covered hundreds of miles preparing for the race. And he'd heard that Bart Bummer had imported some wonderful dogs for the event. *But he won't find one like Big Fella,* Max thought. When Bart heard that Max was replacing an ailing Jake Mitchell as driver, he had scoffed at the chances of Max winning—or even coming close. That had made Max even more determined.

"The Mitchell kid is still wet behind the ears," Bart had told his buddies. "And he's driving Jake Mitchell's team of mutts. They're old and slower than fat-bellied turtles. What's more, even old mutts know when a musher is nervous and new to the trail. They won't run a lick for someone like that."

When he returned at mid-morning, Max took Marty aside. "I think Emily and Jake need some time together. You know, to catch up on things. Why don't you go into town while I run the dogs? I'll meet you downtown later—at the Bo Peep."

"I was planning to go into town, anyway," Marty said. "And I've got to hurry because I want to win first prize money in the fishing derby and the pie-eating contest."

Max looked at his watch. "You can't possibly win the fishing derby. The contest opened on Monday and it closes at noon today. You'll only have a couple of hours to outfish some of the best anglers in the North Country."

"Don't worry about me, brother. I know there's a big fish waiting under the ice for me to show up. He'll be nice and hungry when I get there. I just hope I can carry him to the judge's table—all by myself."

Max grinned and said, "If he's that big, just be careful he doesn't pull you through the hole in the ice instead of the other way around."

Before he left for town, Marty rummaged around in the barn. When he came out, he was carrying some of Uncle Jake's fishing gear. He thought how pleased and surprised Max and Uncle Jake—and Emily too—would be when he came home with the first prize money. But Max was right about one thing. He didn't have much time. The fishing derby would close at noon. He began to jog. He'd have only two hours on the lake. The fish had better be hungry for what he had to offer.

To make it easy on the derby entrants, holes had been augured through the foot-thick ice of the lake. Marty found one of the holes unattended and broke the thin shell ice that had already frozen over it. Some distance away, another fisherman was working a hole. He appeared to be about Marty's age but a bright red parka covered most of his face and Marty couldn't really see his features. Marty called out, "Hello there! Any luck?" but he got no answer. The other fellow didn't move. He seemed not to hear, intent on catching a fish. Marty shrugged, baited his line and went to work. He leaned over and put his face to the hole. Then he crooned, "Here, fishy, fishy. Here, fishy, fishy." He looked around, fearful that someone would hear him. Marty believed the secret to good fishing was luring the fish to the bait with soothing words.

"Here, fishy, fishy. Here, fishy, fishy."

After a few minutes he started to become bored. And he was cold. Reaching out, he pulled the line up and down, hoping to attract a big walleye or pike. Half an hour went by. Nothing happened. Farther out in the lake, he saw men in cozy little cabins or huts made especially for ice fishing. Those men have the right idea, he thought. They stay nice and warm inside a hut while I'm freezing my butt off.

"Here, fishy, fishy."

Just then, he felt a tug on his line. Then another tug, this one stronger. He held tightly to his line, but the fish was strong and pulled Marty's hand and arm into the hole, soaking his jacket. "Holy smoke!" Marty said aloud. "I've got me a beauty."

Instinctively he began yanking the line in, using both hands, and using all of his strength. Up through the hole came a huge walleye, fighting the hook, flipping and flopping and sending a spray of cold water all over Marty. Marty didn't care. He'd landed a whopper and he laughed out loud while the big fish flopped its life away on the ice in front of him. Marty put one boot on the fish to keep it still. Then he lifted it by the gills and examined it closely.

"It's the biggest fish I've ever caught," he murmured. "Look! Look!" he shouted at the fisherman in the red parka, standing at the nearby hole. The other fisherman stole a glance at Marty, waved congratulations and turned back to his fishing hole. Marty was well satisfied with his catch. The fishing derby would close in half an hour and he'd better get his entry in on time. He picked up his gear and ran to the community centre where he plopped his walleye on the scales.

"Twelve pounds, two ounces," intoned the keeper of the scales. "Nice catch, son. That's the biggest walleye we've seen so far." He glanced at the schoolhouse clock on the wall. "And just fifteen minutes to go. Looks like you're going to be a winner."

Marty beamed and took a chair. He was fifteen minutes away from winning one hundred dollars. "Oh, boy!"

He kept glancing at the clock on the wall, the minute hand crawling around like a dopey snail. Ten minutes to noon. Five minutes to noon.

With two minutes to closing time in the derby, a slim figure wearing a big red parka slipped through the door. Marty sat straight up in his chair. He was apprehensive. It was Red Parka, the fisherman he'd seen on the lake, the one who'd been standing not far away from him.

Red Parka approached the scales, reached into a cloth bag and bounced a large walleye onto the scales, making them quiver. Marty quivered too when he heard the results.

"Twelve pounds and...eight ounces."

Somewhere a bell clanged, signalling the end of the fishing derby. From the window, Marty could see a few fishermen trudging in from the frozen lake. None of them were lugging twelve pounders, he could see that. It meant that Red Parka had won first prize—at the very last second.

Marty stood up, his mouth agape. He couldn't believe it. A guy had marched in at the last minute and grabbed first prize away from him. Now people were patting the young man on the back. Someone was pressing five twenty-dollar bills in his hand. "Darn it all," grumbled Marty disconsolately. "I gotta be a good sport about this," he told himself.

The derby winner pulled off his parka. Marty gasped. The winner was not a he at all, he...was a...she! A girl with large blue eyes and long blonde hair.

Marty was still in shock when she walked up to him. "I'm sorry it was you I beat," she graciously said. "You caught a wonderful fish and I saw how happy you were when you landed it. Mine came along just a few minutes later and it was just a teeny bit bigger."

Her smile was dazzling. Marty had no idea what to say. All he could do was stare into her amazing blue eyes.

"Hello?" she teased, waving a hand in front of his dazed face.

"Uh, that's fishing," he mumbled stupidly. "My uncle says it pays to be patient. Well, that's you. Patience paid off today. Congratulations."

"My name's Melissa," she said, "and I've got a whole lot of money in my pocket. The least I can do is offer to buy you some burgers and fries at the Bo Peep. How about it?"

"My name's Marty," he replied, extending his hand. He was glad he'd remembered to wash up after handling his fish. "And I'd be delighted to have a burger with you, Melissa. But just a small one. I'm entering the pie-eating contest in an hour and I've got to save some room."

"We'll have to hurry," Melissa said. "I promised my aunt I'd help her work on one of the ice statues this afternoon."

CHAPTER 8

MARTY ENTERS AN
EATING EVENT

Back at Uncle Jake's place Max gave the sled dogs a rest. He put them in their pen and checked their water supply. "Look after your team, boy," he told Big Fella. "You're their leader now." Max closed the gate.

Max hoped Marty was having a good time in town but he worried that he might run into the Bummer boys. Surely they wouldn't pick on someone like Marty, someone younger and smaller than themselves. But he wouldn't put it past them.

He went into the house and saw a note from Emily on the kitchen table.

Dear Max: I took Uncle Jake into town in the truck. Dr. Green gave his permission. We are going to work on the ice sculpture. My niece will be there to help. Then we're going to watch the dog weight pull competition. Come by and see us. Emily.

Max made himself a peanut butter sandwich and washed it down with a glass of milk. He washed up, changed his clothes and went back out to the dog pen. He watched Big Fella scampering and playing with the other dogs. Then Big Fella saw Max standing by the gate. He loped over and began licking his hand through the fence. Max leaned over and had a talk with the husky. "Listen, pal. I can't decide whether or not to enter you in the dog weight pull event today. It would be a shame if you pulled too hard and injured a muscle or something. I want you in peak condition for the big race on Saturday. What do you think?"

Big Fella barked and shook his head. Max laughed. "Is that a yes? Well, both Dad and Uncle Jake seem to think you'll be fine. You might even win the event." Big Fella looked so eager to accompany Max into town that Max couldn't resist. He opened the gate and said, "All right. Come on then." They hurried into Storm Valley.

Main Street was gaily decorated with balloons and sparkling lights. In the park, the high school band played lively airs. They passed the noisy Storm Valley Hotel, which was so crowded with revellers that some were sleeping on cots in the hallways.

"I hear the mattresses are so lumpy that some of the miners would rather sleep on the floor," Uncle Jake had once said. "And the snoring is so loud a lot of the residents wear ear muffs when they go to bed." Uncle Jake had insisted it was the honest truth, causing Max and Marty to roll their eyes.

Now Max began to think there was some truth in what Uncle Jake had said. The laughter and chatter, the high-pitched buzz of many conversations emanating from the hotel's restaurant, could be heard for blocks around. He remembered something else Uncle Jake had mentioned. "Late at night," he had said, "when the band begins to play and a sing-along begins, and the cloggers get to dancing, miners and trappers living all along the lakeshore will jump from their beds, either to complain about the 'gold-erned noise' or to throw on their clothes and come join the fun. Most times it's to join in the fun."

Prospectors and lumberjacks were in town, down from the north—from Burnt Bacon Creek, Happy Landing and Mabel's Mine. Trappers came in from the bush and all were there for a few days of fun and friendly competition. They'd determine who could climb a tall pole the fastest, who could split a sturdy log with axe or saw in a matter of seconds, who would be crowned "champion arm wrestler" and "fastest man on snowshoes."

Max saw what he was looking for; a big sign outside the town hall—Pie Eating Contest Today—and he darted inside. "This is where I'll find Marty," he told himself. Sure enough, his brother was sitting at a long table with his sleeves rolled up. He was elbow to elbow with a dozen other men. At the end of the table, Babe and Brutus Bummer shot Max a dirty look.

"Hey, Max! Hi, Big Fella!" Marty shouted, waving them over. "Watch me win this contest. Cost me a dollar to enter. Why don't you sit in? The contest is open to everyone."

Dozens of home-baked apple pies lined the table and the smell in the room had the onlookers licking their lips.

"Marty, I can't. I just had lunch."

"So did I," Marty grinned. "A young lady bought me lunch."

"You're kidding. Who was she?"

"I'll tell you later. Contest is about to start."

Max leaned over his brother's shoulder. "If you just had lunch, you'll never win this contest. What did you have to eat?"

"Not much. A burger and fries, a glass of milk. And an ice cream sundae. I couldn't resist. Melissa paid for everything."

"Melissa?"

"Yeah, Melissa. A girl I met. She beat me in the fishing derby but only by this much." He held up his thumb and index fingers and held them almost together. "Tell you more later."

A bell rang and the apple-pie eaters dived in. The

contestants swallowed great gobs of apple and crust. Huge chunks seemed to disappear down open throats without the bother of being chewed. Bits of crust and apple dropped onto laps, into beards and onto the floor. Max could see that his brother Marty, although game, was badly overmatched. Some of these lumberjacks and miners were known throughout the North Country for their voracious appetites.

A giant of a lumberjack, Ernie "Too Tall" Thomas, swallowed pie after pie like an unstoppable eating machine. When others had quit, stuffed beyond capacity, he polished off another and then one more, calmly wiping his hands on his plaid shirt, which was already liberally spotted with pie crust, ketchup, mustard and gravy stains.

When whole pies disappeared, others replaced them. In half an hour it was all over. Men quit with slabs of pie wedged from their mouths. Max saw Babe Bummer gag and fall to the floor. Brutus put his head down on the table and the side of his face landed in a plate with half a pie on it.

Marty, his cheeks puffed out, had reached for another piece of pie and had it halfway to his face when he surrendered. He slid off his chair and, clutching his stomach, sat on the floor.

Too Tall belched so thunderously it rattled the pie plates on the table. He smiled contentedly and asked a pie-maker, "You gals make great pie. Now could I trouble one of you for a glass of milk to wash it all down?"

Marty clamped both hands over his mouth and rushed to the bathroom. There was a lineup. He dashed outside and up-chucked into some bushes.

Max found him there, groaning miserably, one hand to his mouth, the other to his stomach. Big Fella stood back, watching Marty curiously. Max imagined him thinking that people put the most amazing things in their stomachs—and so much of it. They eat and fall down; they drink and fall down. And they call us dumb animals. Well, most animals I know are a lot smarter than that.

"Here," Max said, handing Marty a fistful of dollar bills.

"What's that for?" Marty said, turning to up-chuck once more, startling birds from a nearby tree.

"They awarded you a consolation prize," Max said. "Ten bucks. It's for the entrant who ate the least amount of pie. It's a kind of booby prize. And you won it. Congratulations."

A few minutes later, Marty felt a bit better. The money he'd won had brought a smile back to his face. The boys walked on down the hill toward the lake. "I still feel like there's a bowling ball rolling around in my belly," Marty complained. He winced, "I think the pins are in there too. Oh, oh, somebody just scored a strike."

"Hey, there's Uncle Jake and Emily," Max said, "They're working on an ice sculpture. And there's someone helping them out."

They marvelled at what they saw. Their Uncle Jake, with his artist's eye and with Emily's help, had chiselled out a splendid statue of a huge walrus.

"Wait a minute, Max." Marty tugged on his brother's arm. "That's Melissa helping them," he whispered. "What's she doing here?"

"So that's Melissa? The girl who bought you lunch. I hope you showed good table manners."

"Oh, I did. For the most part, anyway. Just as we got up from the table I let go an awful belch. Couldn't help it. Everybody in the Bo Peep turned to look and I said, 'Excuse me, folks.' Melissa just giggled. Then we ran out the door. But it could have been worse."

"How could it have been worse?"

"Well, while we were eating, I felt a huge fart coming on. But I held it in. Honest I did. Melissa wouldn't have thought that was so funny, I bet."

Max winced. "You're almost as bad as the awful Bummers." Then he asked, "How was it losing to a girl?"

"All right," said Marty. "You don't mind losing to a girl when she's the best looking girl in town."

Uncle Jake and Emily greeted them and Melissa gave them a big smile. Emily said, "Boys, I want you to meet my niece Melissa. She came along to lend a hand. Did you know she won the fishing contest today?"

Marty spoke up. "I know she did because I finished second. And Melissa bought me a burger. But I didn't know she was your niece, Emily."

Uncle Jake finished chiselling out the nose of the walrus and chuckled. "Life is full of surprises, isn't it? Emily has been Melissa's guardian for several years now and has been doing a great job of it, too. Right Melissa?"

Melissa nodded her head enthusiastically. "Aunt Emily is the best thing ever to happen to me—since the car accident I mean. I love her to death. But then, everybody does. Right, Uncle Jake?"

Uncle Jake laughed and put down his chisel. "I'm not really your uncle, Melissa. But I like it when you call me that. And yes, everybody loves Emily." He gave Emily a look that spoke volumes and then changed the subject. "Say, we were just going to head over to the Bo Peep for a snack. Care to join us?"

The thought of more food turned Marty's complexion an odious green. "No thanks," he groaned. "I'm thinking of going on a diet."

Max also declined the invitation and asked if they could be of any help on the sculpture?

"Nope. Almost finished," said Uncle Jake. "Emily

and Melissa did most of the work and we're almost done. Looks pretty good if I do say so."

Max was genuinely impressed with his uncle's skill with the chisel. "It looks great, Uncle Jake. First prize for sure."

"We'll see about that. Why don't you boys take Melissa with you and see some of the sights?"

"I was going to enter Big Fella in the sled weight pull," Max said. "What do you think?"

"Well, do it, nephew. Competition starts in a few minutes on the lake. Better get going. Good luck, Big Fella."

"Hey, that's a great idea," Marty said enthusiastically. "Let's get Big Fella down there. Unless you'd rather go to the Bo Peep, Melissa."

Marty crossed his fingers, hoping she'd say no.

"No, thanks," she answered. "I'd rather go with you, Marty." She turned back to Marty and then put her hand to her mouth, trying to hold back more giggling. "Besides," she said, "I'm not sure they'll let us back in the Bo Peep after your performance in there today."

CHAPTER 9

BIG FELLA PULLS HIS WEIGHT

At least two hundred curious people turned out for the dog weight pull event on Thursday afternoon. It was a new event. Doc Green, who was there to assure no cruelty to animals was involved, spoke into a megaphone, explaining the rules.

"Half a dozen dogs are entered in this event," he said. "They'll start from behind a line drawn on the ice. The dogs will be rigged to a sled one at a time and the sled will be filled with hundred-pound sacks of grain. The event will begin with a minimum load of fifteen hundred pounds, because all of these dogs are very strong."

"By the way," he added, "the world record holder—Coalfoot—once dragged two thousand pounds, an amazing feat for a dog. We don't expect to get close to that record today."

"How far will they have to pull the load?" someone asked.

"Each dog has one minute in which to pull the sled twenty-five feet," Doc Green explained. "You can see where we've marked the finish line on the ice with blue paint. Our first entrant is Luther. Ready, Luther?"

A big Labrador rigged to the sled barked twice and everybody laughed.

The starter blew his whistle. His owner bellowed, "Go, Luther!" and Luther lunged forward. Slowly the weighted sled crept forward and then stopped. It had progressed only a foot or two when Luther stopped and yawned. Then he lay down on the ice. His owner, a local miner, stood at the finish line making frantic hand signals. He was barred by the rules from calling to his dog or lending any kind of vocal encouragement—except at the start of the pull. Then he could shout, "Go!" or "Here, boy!" or "Hike!" or even "Take a hike!" Three words only. But he could wave his dog toward him or roll his eyes at him or slap his knee. He could even stand on his head if he thought that would help. But he wasn't allowed to carry food of any kind to entice his dog by the smell. But Luther wasn't interested in pulling a stupid old sled any farther. He didn't care that he was breaking his owner's heart. The whistle blew and he was quickly released, showing no shame whatsoever. The heavy sled was backed into position on the starting line and another dog took his place.

It was Bart Bummer's prized dog Bullseye, a sturdy Siberian. "Put another couple of sacks on the sled," Bart told the starter. "Bullseye ain't no wimpy Labrador. He'll pull seventeen hundred pounds, I'll betcha."

And Bullseye did. Bart shouted, "Come on, Bullseye!" and the dog strained at the harness until spectators began to say "oooh," certain it would snap. But the leather held and Bullseye, every muscle in his body quivering, pulled the sled for twenty-five feet in fifty-two seconds.

"I'd like to see any dog top that," Bart bragged.

Three more dogs challenged Bullseye. Another Labrador showed great strength and pulled the seventeen-hundred-pound sled over the course but he missed the one-minute time limit by ten seconds and was disqualified.

The other two, both mixed breeds, failed to get the sled started at all at that weight.

Max held Big Fella by his leash. He was undecided. Sure, it would be embarrassing if his husky couldn't move the sled. But mostly, he didn't want Big Fella to hurt himself. Uncle Jake had assured him that sled dogs were bred to carry weights on sleds and thrived on such challenges. Even so...

Max felt a nudge in the back from Marty. "What are you waiting for? Get Big Fella up there."

"How about it, young man?" the starter barked. "Your dog's next."

Bart Bummer stepped forward, his hand out for the prize money. "Looks like Mitchell is backing out," he said with a laugh. "It takes a real dog to win this event. So I'll take my prize money and be off."

Big Fella looked up beseechingly at Max.

"All right!" Max shouted at the starter. "Let's start at seventeen hundred pounds."

The crowd whooped. They didn't want Bart Bummer to win the prize money without a battle.

Big Fella was placed in the harness and Max took his position just beyond the finish line. He smiled encouragingly at Big Fella. The whistle blew. Max yelled, "Hike! Hike!" Big Fella strained at the harness, his head down, and his claws digging into the ice. The sled began to move ever so slowly. Then Big Fella yelped and found a reserve of strength. The sled moved faster. The seconds ticked by on the starter's watch. Ten, twenty, thirty. Big Fella had covered more than half the distance. But could he beat Bullseye's time? The sled was sliding smoothly now and Big Fella was showing amazing endurance and fierce determination. He crossed the line to a huge round of applause, wagging his tail, knowing he'd done well. He welcomed the embraces he received, first from Max, then from Marty and Melissa.

"Good dog! Good dog!" Max crooned. Even he was surprised at Big Fella's performance.

The starter checked his stopwatch. "Folks, we've got a tie. Both Bullseye and Big Fella were timed in fifty-two seconds." He turned to Max and Bart Bummer. "You fellows want to split the prize money?"

"We do not!" Bart fired back. "Put another hundred pounds on that sled."

"But Bart, that's an awful lot of weight. Why not split the money?"

"Split with that kid? He almost killed my boys with his reckless driving," he sneered. "No way! Put another hundred pounds on."

"Okay with you, kid?" the starter asked Max.

"I guess so," Max replied. "But with one condition. No more races after this. It would be too much to ask of any dog."

"Suit yourself," Bart Bummer agreed. He took his place at the finish line. Max noticed that his son Bert joined him there. While Bullseye was being harnessed to the sled, Bert yelled out, "Come on, Bullseye! Are you ready, Bullseye? Let's go, Bullseye!"

The starter glared at him. "Stop that, Bert! An owner must not encourage his dog with verbal commands until the whistle blows. That's a strict rule."

Bert laughed and shot back. "But I'm not the owner. My dad is. I'm just an innocent bystander."

"Just be quiet," the starter commanded, raising his whistle.

At the whistle, Bart yelled, "Come on, Bullllssseye!" Once again, Bullseye showed amazing strength. The extra weight slowed him down some- what but he kept the sled moving at a turtle-like pace. Near the finish line, his head came up. He sniffed the air and suddenly seemed to be inspired, to gain a little momentum. When he crossed the fin- ish line, he ignored Bart and jumped up on Bert Bummer, who rubbed his head and told him what a champion he was.

"Bullseye's time...fifty-nine seconds!" announced the starter. "That's going to be very hard to beat."

As Max led Big Fella to the starting line, the Bummers, father and son, celebrated Bullseye's "winning" performance. They waved to people in the crowd. They doffed their hats and took deep bows. They hugged each other. Most people stand- ing around ignored their theatrics, thinking it unsportsmanlike. After all, the contest wasn't over.

Max went to the finish line. He had to bump Bert off the line. "Excuse me," he said.

"Hey! Watch it!" Bert shot back. But he hustled off, almost guiltily.

That's odd, thought Max. He sniffed the air. What's that smell? Bert hasn't bathed in some time, he guessed. Something had fallen from Bert's pocket into the snow. Max leaned over to see what it was. "It's a big slice of salmon!" he murmured angrily.

"No wonder Bullseye had a big finish and went straight to Bert," he muttered. "I should have known the Bummers couldn't enter a contest without cheating."

Max had to focus.

He caught Big Fella's attention. He winked and grinned. "You can do it," he said, mouthing the words, staying within the rules. Big Fella gave his head a confident shake, as if to say, "You bet I can!"

On the whistle and the command "Hike! Hike!" Big Fella scratched his way forward, his head almost at ice level. Even so, his eyes never left Max. The harness stretched taut and the sled began to move. Max held his breath as it slowly slid along the ice, eighteen hundred pounds of sled being pulled along by a fiercely determined sled dog. The sled appeared to be travelling at about the same rate of speed Bullseye had managed. But who could tell?

Big Fella strained to reach the finish line and Max jumped aside to give him room. It was going to be close.

The crowd roared when Big Fella heaved himself across the line, the sled at his heels.

A hush fell over the spectators. The starter looked at his watch then checked it again. Finally he announced, "The time for Big Fella is...fifty-eight seconds! Big Fella wins by one second!"

There was pandemonium along the lakeshore.

People whooped and hollered and rushed forward to congratulate Max. They gushed over his dog and little children patted the champion husky and hugged him. Big Fella sat there panting, waiting patiently for someone to bring him a drink of water and wondering what all the fuss was about.

Max was elated.

"It's pretty amazing to have a dog like Big Fella," he told a reporter for the local paper. "My brother and I never know what he's going to do next. All we know is we're going to be surprised and happy no matter what he does. I wish every kid could own a dog like ours."

Max went back to the finish line and found the slice of salmon in the snow. He picked it up and went over to where Bart and Bert Bummer were standing, unfairly berating Bullseye, who whined and cringed.

"Hey, Bert," said Max, his hand outstretched. "You dropped this back there."

Bert was stunned for a moment. In false surprise he said, "Oh, yeah. Part of the sandwich I made for lunch. I musta dropped it somewhere."

Max tossed the chunk of salmon high toward Bullseye, who swallowed it greedily.

"You earned it, boy," Max said, walking away. Bullseye barked gratefully.

CHAPTER 10

THE SKATING RACE

The crowd began to move farther down the shoreline to join a much bigger crowd gathered around the dock.

"What's up?" asked Marty. "Why are there so many people here?"

"By gosh, it's the skating races," replied Max, slapping the side of his head. "I got so busy with the sled dogs this morning and the weight pulling event after that, I forgot all about them. I even forgot to bring my skates. They're back at Uncle Jake's."

"I'll run back and get them," Marty said. "It's only half a mile there and back. It looks like the races are just getting underway and the little kids will be first, the senior events later. We've got time."

"All right. And take Big Fella with you. Give him some food and water and put him in the dog pen. He needs to rest up for Saturday's race."

Marty was off like a rocket, Big Fella, on the leash,

scampering along beside him. Max and Melissa made their way down to the dock on the lake.

"Melissa, it looks like you've completely captivated my young brother."

"He's a great guy," she answered with a smile. "How did he do in the pie-eating contest? I forgot to ask him."

"Well, he won ten dollars, " Max answered. "And he probably won't eat apple pie again for the rest of his life."

A group of young men were gathered on the ice beside the dock. They had their skates on and they were warming up for the main event. All five of the Bummer brothers were in the group. Max was tempted to turn and go back, to avoid any kind of confrontation. But he took a deep breath and stepped onto the dock, Melissa right behind him.

From the ice below, Brutus and Babe spotted him. "There he is," Brutus shouted, pointing. He motioned his brothers to come closer. "The numbskull Mitchell kid who almost killed Babe and me."

Brutus sneered and flapped his arms like a bird. "I thought you were going to race against us, Mitchell, but I see you've chickened out. Don't tell us you forgot your skates."

"They're on their way," Max replied, "I'll see you gents at the starting line."

"That your girlfriend or are you baby sitting today?" Brutus sneered.

Max was suddenly angry. But he felt Melissa's hand on his sleeve. "Just ignore them, Max. Don't let them get your goat."

He smiled at her. "You're right, Melissa." He turned his back on the Bummer boys and went over to check with the starter. Then he and Melissa mingled with the crowd. After twenty minutes there was still no sign of Marty and Max was getting worried.

"Good luck, kid," said a burly bearded man in a red mackinaw, clapping Max on the shoulder, almost crushing a few bones. Max recognized him as "Too Tall" Thomas, winner of the pie-eating contest. Max noticed there were still small pieces of piecrust lodged in his beard. The big man was eating a pizza and some of the sauce had dripped onto his plaid shirt. "You don't know me, kid, but I saw you stand up to the Bummer boys the other day. That took real guts. And I was real happy to see your great-looking dog win the pulling contest over Bart Bummer's dog. Too bad such a fine animal is stuck with such a low-down-no-account owner. Now you've got to beat his no-good kids on the ice today. Watch them. They don't play fair. And then comes your big test on Saturday in the derby. Make it a hat trick, eh, kid? I've been waiting a long time for someone to come along and put a sock in Bart Bummer's big mouth."

"Thanks, mister," said Max. "I'll do my best."

"Sure you will." He swatted Max on the back in a

friendly way. It was like being hit with a baseball bat. Max staggered forward. "See you later, pal," said the giant. "Now go and win that race."

"Too Tall" Thomas moved away and people scurried out of his path when they saw him coming. He was hungry and was seeking food and refreshment at the temporary lunch counter someone had set up near the dock.

Suddenly, the crowd surged forward. The starter, barking through a megaphone, called the senior skaters to the starting line.

"Hey, Mitchell!" yelled Brutus. "Are you in or are you out?"

"He's in! And he's going to whip your butt." It was Marty. He'd arrived with the skates and thrust them at Max. "Quick! Put them on. You've only got a minute."

"What kept you?" Max asked his brother.

Marty whispered in Max's ear, so Melissa wouldn't hear. "I had to go to the bathroom once and I threw up twice. I'll never eat apple pie again as long as I live."

"I figured as much," Max answered.

Max ran to the dock and threw on his skates. The starter looked over and gave him a few extra seconds to get ready. There was no time for a warm-up.

"Come on. Let's go!" Brutus shouted, scowling at the starter.

Max was still scrambling onto the ice when the gun went off and two dozen skaters sped away from the starting line. Within seconds, elbows flying, the Bummer brothers were muscling their way to the front of the pack. A slight, fast skater went down, sandwiched by two of the Bummer boys. Their victim struck his head on the ice but the Bummers showed no sympathy. They looked back and laughed.

Max leaped over the fallen skater and attempted to catch up to the others. His muscles felt stiff and his stride was uneven. The lake ice had been cleaned of snow by a tractor with a large blade in front, but there were big cracks to worry about. Catch a skate blade in one of those and he could fall and break an ankle.

At the half-mile mark, Max began to feel better. He had developed a rhythm and his strides had lengthened. He placed his hands behind his back like he'd seen the top speed skaters do and it seemed to relax him. He began to gain on the front-runners.

Ahead, he saw one of the Bummer brothers begin to falter. *That'll be Bert*, Max thought. *Heavy smoker. And a drinker too. Starting to lose his hair. And with that potbelly, he won't have the stamina to finish. But the other ones might.*

At the end of a mile, the skaters rounded a red oil drum anchored in the ice. As each skater leaned in to make the turn, chunks of ice and snow flew from his blades. Bert Bummer started around the drum on rubbery legs. Then he lost his balance, hit the drum with his lower body and somersaulted through the air. He came down on his back and shoulders and skidded across the ice. With the breath knocked out of him, he sat up, red-faced and exhausted, and began to cough. Max waved at him as he skated by.

The return journey was into the wind and the skaters slowed noticeably. Max was pumping hard, gaining ground and with half a mile to go he was up among the leaders. He made a move to pass Billy Bummer. Billy threw out an elbow to impede Max, but Billy was too weary to put much effort into it. Then Billy swerved in front of Max and tried to trip him. Max leaned into him with a shoulder, like he'd done hundreds of times in hockey games. The jolt knocked Billy right off his skates. His legs buckled, his arms flew up and he hit the ice hard, landing on his behind. "Nice try, Billy!" Max said as he flashed by. Billy banged both fists on the ice and swore at Max in frustration.

"Such naughty language, Billy. Shame on you."

Billy howled a reply Max didn't hear and didn't care to hear. He lowered his head and skated on, refusing to look back, a big smile on his face.

Max scooted around a flagging skater and looked up just in time to avoid a collision. Boris Bummer had suddenly slowed in front of Max and his trailing skate clipped Max on the shinbone. A stabbing pain shot through his leg, throwing him offstride. Boris glanced back, a twisted grin on his face. "Stay back or I'll cut your legs off at the knees!" he shouted. But Boris was breathing hard. He was almost spent and Max figured his threat was mostly bluff. Max decided to circle around him, going wide to avoid a straight-arm, a flying elbow or other Bummer trick. And was soon glad that he did. Out of the corner of his eye, he saw some small objects spill onto the ice and they were coming from Boris' pant legs. Pennies! Boris had one hand in his pocket and was dropping a handful of pennies through a hole in his pocket. They fell down his pant leg and hit the ice, bouncing in front of the skaters who trailed him. Max had no doubt they were intended to trip him up. If Max stepped on one of the coins, he would go down heavily and perhaps be badly injured. Fortunately, he had given Boris a wide berth when he passed him but the teenager coming up behind was not so lucky. His skate hit one of the coins and he fell awkwardly, clutching his ankle and crying out in pain. By then Max had sped past Boris and left him well behind.

Through his shredded pant leg, Max could feel the blood dripping down his leg. He ignored the pain in his leg, found his stride and moved up again. Just ahead, he saw a gap open up between the leaders, Brutus and Babe, who were skating abreast of each other. The brothers left an inviting alley for anyone to scoot through if they were coming from behind. Max was suspicious. *Perhaps that gap is a little too inviting*, he thought.

With two hundred yards to go, the remaining skaters began to sprint. The pace was frantic—an all-out dash to the finish line. Max could hear the crowd on shore cheering. He used his arms now to assist his legs, just like he did on the hockey rink. And he sped straight toward the opening between Brutus and Babe.

Fifty yards to go. The roar of the crowd was deafening and it echoed off the hills and across the ice. Babe and Brutus sneaked glances back at Max.

His dash between them was precisely what they expected and gleefully they closed the gap between them when Max flew into their trap.

But Max had a plan of his own. He saw the elbows come up; he saw the shoulders close in like pincers. In another second he'd be trapped and bounced to the ice. It was then that he made his move—a bold move. Just when it appeared he'd be smashed to the ice by the Bummers, he accelerated.

His burst of speed, held in reserve until now, carried him between the Bummer brothers and to open ice just as the trap behind him closed with a thud but without a victim. The Bummer brothers collided, not with Max, but with each other. They howled in frustration as they bodychecked each other to the hard ice, bouncing and rolling on their backs and their bellies toward the finish line but not quite reaching it. Max flashed across the line ahead of them and raised his arms in victory. When he skidded to a stop, he acknowledged the cheers of the crowd; aware that most of the spectators were genuinely happy to see him beat the Bummer boys. The cheering and hand clapping lasted for several minutes.

Then Marty was there beside him, grabbing him in his arms and pounding him on the back. Melissa added her congratulations. The crowd gathered around him and people shook his hand.

"Too Tall" Thomas, chewing on a huge sandwich, fought his way through. "You made us proud, boy," he said, around a mouthful of ham and cheese. "We've waited a long time to see those Bummer's take a beating."

The man with the megaphone stood on the dock and addressed the spectators, many of whom were still applauding the young skater's sterling effort.

"Folks, you saw the thrilling finish to a thrilling race. And the winner of the senior skating race—and in record time—is Max Mitchell. That's Jake Mitchell's nephew, folks, and this lad is a real champion. It's a pleasure to award him first prize money of one hundred dollars. Come and get it, son."

After he accepted his prize money, Max made a little thank-you speech. And when he looked out over the crowd he spotted a familiar face, a face beaming with pride, in the back row. It was Uncle Jake. He waved one arm; the other was locked firmly in Emily's.

"Congratulations, nephew," Uncle Jake shouted. "You skated a great race."

Marty assisted in helping Max out of his skates, thinking he couldn't have wished for a better brother.

Max turned to leave and almost bumped into Babe Bummer. Babe had a strange look on his face, as if he wanted to say something but didn't know how to say it. His mouth opened and closed several times but no words came out. Finally he blurted out, "Nice race." Then he turned and hurried away.

"Wasn't that strange?" Max asked, turning back to Marty.

"You mean, what he said? Sure was," Marty agreed. He turned to look after Babe and shrugged. "I guess it proves even a Bummer can say something nice once in awhile. Even after he tried to knock you on your butt."

CHAPTER 11

BEAR WRESTLING

After everyone made a big fuss over Max for his thrilling victory in the senior skating race, Uncle Jake and Emily decided to drive over to the arena to watch some of the curling matches.

"We'll stay here if you don't mind," Max said. "Marty and I are not big fans of curling."

"Yeah, sliding rocks along the ice and using brooms to sweep them into a house doesn't make much sense to me," Marty added.

"We know a lot of people who think it's a great game," Uncle Jake said. "Some day maybe you will too. Some of our friends are competing so we'll go see how they're doing. Semifinals are today and tomorrow—the final match on Saturday. Give me your skates, Max. I'll throw them in the truck. I'll bring them home for you."

When Max handed him his skates, Uncle Jake slipped a few dollars into his hand. "You three kids have a treat or two on me," he said with a grin. "Save your prize money from the skating race. And get Melissa home at a decent hour."

In the town park, opposite the band shell, the three teenagers noticed a crowd gathering and they hurried over to investigate. "Hey, it's the bear wrestling contest," Marty said. "This should be fun."

"There's Bert and Boris Bummer over there," said Max. "I'm sure they'll be entered. It only makes sense the dumbest event would attract the dumbest contestants."

"There's the bear," Melissa said, pointing. "He's a mangy old thing. How sad. He looks so miserable."

"He scared the heck out of us back on the train," Marty said. "But he doesn't look like he could hurt a fly, really."

"Well," Melissa said, "I think this event is awful. And cruel." Max and Marty nodded in agreement.

Snow had been scraped away from the ground and piled up in banks to form an area for the wrestling. It was something like a boxing ring but with no posts or ropes. Bert Bummer immediately jumped over a bank of snow and whistled at the bear. "Come on, old bub. Let's see what you've got."

The bear looked bored. He had a long chain around his neck and the end of the chain was tied to the trunk of a nearby tree. Under his leather muzzle he seemed to sigh. "He looks more worn out than dangerous." Marty said. "Still, I wonder if anybody would challenge him if he wasn't wearing that muzzle."

"Poor thing," Melissa said. "He looks like he wishes he was hibernating out in the woods somewhere. It can't be much fun for him—being forced to wrestle some big lumberjack."

"His owner takes him from town to town and there's a hundred dollars reward to anyone who can pin him for ten seconds," Max explained. "The bear weighs about four hundred pounds so I guess he doesn't get pinned very often. "

"Look," Marty said, "the match is beginning. Looks like Bert Bummer thinks he can put the old bear down."

The bear eyed Bert Bummer warily as he approached. Bert moved boldly at the bear and got one arm around his thick neck. But when he tried to throw him to the ground, the bear tossed its head, breaking Bert's hold. The bear parried with a swipe of a big paw but Bert pranced aside, grinning. He slapped the bear on the top of his head, to show he was in charge.

"That man makes me angry. He's nothing but a big show-off," Melissa snorted.

"You're not the only one he makes angry," warned Max. Indeed, the gentle bear had been roused to anger by Bert's foolish taunting. Bert dashed in and looped one arm under the bear's right front leg, then heaved. The bear, caught off balance, crashed to the ground. A half growl, half moan came from its throat.

"Gotcha now!" teased Bert. He leaped on top of the bear. If Bert could pin him there for ten seconds, he would pocket an easy one hundred dollars.

But the canny bear sprang to his feet and easily shook Bert off. He slapped Bert with a blow to the chest. It sent Bert reeling. Stunned, Bert toppled backwards into a snowbank. Many in the crowd howled in delight.

Boris Bummer, his face red with anger, rushed over and helped his brother to his feet. While he was brushing snow from Bert, Boris slipped Bert some heavy workmen's mitts.

"Those mitts are as big as boxing gloves," Max said to Marty and Melissa. "There's something fishy about this."

With renewed confidence, Bert approached the bear. He darted in and struck hard at the bear's throat. The bear howled in rage. Bert hit him again and the bear pedalled back. Boris raised his big boot and stamped hard on the bear's paw. Again the bear howled in misery.

The bear's owner stepped forward. "Wait!" he cried out. "You wrestle my bear, you don't beat him to death. And you don't stomp on his foot."

Boris shoved the owner back. "Stay out of this, old man!" he said, enraged.

Bert punched the bear several more times with the gloves. The bear's anguished cries brought people running to the scene.

"I think those mitts have something in them, Max!" Marty said.

Max could take it no longer. "Come on, Marty," he said, leaping over a snowbank and charging straight at big Bert Bummer. Max hit Bert so hard with his shoulder that it knocked the breath out of the bigger man. Bert fell flat on his back. Before he could recover, Max had his arms pinned to the ground in a powerful grip.

Bert couldn't move but his brother could. Howling in anger, Boris charged at Max. But he tripped over something—Marty's outstretched foot and sprawled flat on his face in the slush and snow.

"You pipsqueak," he growled, getting to his feet and clawing snow from his eyes. He snarled at Marty. "Say a prayer because I'm gonna kill you, kid."

Marty gamely held up his fists, like a bantamweight boxer, getting ready to defend himself against Jack Dempsey. Even so, he knew he was in for a beating. But before Boris could throw a punch, before he could even raise his big fist, he found himself locked in an embrace. Two arms thrown around his chest, arms much stronger than his own, held him in a vice-like grip. He twisted to look over his shoulder and found himself staring up into the cold blue eyes of Ernie "Too Tall" Thomas.

"You hit that pup and I'll do you some serious damage," the giant lumberjack threatened. "The same goes for you, Bert," who was just now beginning to catch his breath and was struggling under the weight of Max. "Too Tall" nodded at Max. "You can let him up now, son. He gives you any trouble, I've got some pals in the crowd who'd like to have a crack at anyone named Bummer."

Bert rolled out from under Max and struggled to his feet. He put one arm to his shoulder. "I think the Mitchell kid broke something in there," he whined to the crowd.

"Too bad," said "Too Tall," showing no sympathy. "He should have hit you on the head. There's nothing in there. Whatever he did, you had it coming. Now you and Boris get on home before somebody calls Chief Connolly and charges you with cruelty to animals." "Too Tall" released his hold on Boris and the two brothers shuffled away. Someone in the crowd booed them. Another shouted, "Good riddance!"

"Too Tall" shook Max by the hand. "What made you and your brother do a thing like that?" he asked, implying it wasn't the wisest decision they'd ever made. "The Bummer boys might have beaten you and Marty to a pulp."

Max agreed. "There was something odd about the fight," he said. "Seems to me the bear was being abused."

"I knew it!" shouted Marty. "Look at this!" Marty held up a heavy mitt. "Bert lost his mitt when Max flattened him." He held the mitt upside down and a thick coin roll fell onto the ground.

"Why, the sonofagun cheated. He was using loaded gloves," said "Too Tall" Thomas.

"And his mean old brother kept stomping on the bear's paw," Melissa said, indignantly.

Doc Green muscled his way through the crowd. "I told you this was a cruel event," he barked. "Now let's get a vet over here to examine this bear. He may be injured."

He turned on the owner angrily. "I suggest you find a nice zoo somewhere for your bear. He won't survive if you put him back in his natural home— the wilderness."

"Now, wait a minute," the bear's owner protested.

"No, you wait a moment," roared Doc Green. He turned back to the crowd. "This bear's wrestling days are over. As Health Director of this town I declare this event closed. For good! Now let's look forward to Saturday's sled dog races and the windup dance on Saturday night."

"He handled that well," Max said of Doc Green as they walked back across the park.

"Sure did," Marty agreed. "And so did 'Too Tall' Thomas. Hey, Max, I didn't know there was a big dance on Saturday night. Uh...Melissa. Want to go?"

"I'd love to, Marty. But I didn't know you were a dancer."

"Sure am. I'm just as graceful on the dance floor as I am on the ice rink," he boasted.

There was a long patch of ice directly in front of them and Max took a run and slid across it expertly. Melissa followed suit and her slide was even longer. Marty was next. He ran and slid but his foot hit a rut in the ice and he flew off the slick surface and landed headfirst in a snowbank. "See how graceful my brother is," Max said to Melissa. "If you're going to dance with him, be sure you wear a helmet and some shin pads."

"Maybe I'll wear some lumberjack boots as well," laughed Melissa. "You know, the ones with the metal toes."

CHAPTER 12

BIG FELLA GOES MISSING

It was getting dark and time to leave the Carnival grounds. Melissa said she'd have to go home, that her Aunt Emily would probably be at their small apartment by now. Marty said he'd walk her there.

"Want to come, Max?"

Max declined and saw Marty breathe a sigh of relief. Of course, Marty didn't want his brother along when he walked Melissa home.

Max walked back to Uncle Jake's house, hands in his pockets, whistling a happy tune. He was excited about competing in the sled dog race on Saturday and hoped that he and Big Fella would do well and not embarrass themselves.

He found Uncle Jake in the kitchen.

"We just got back from the curling," Uncle Jake said. "Emily drove me home in the truck and then walked back to get dinner ready for Melissa. How about a cup of tea?"

While Max poured water in the kettle, Uncle Jake read the sports page of the local paper.

"Lookee here, Max," he said. "The local sports editor took a poll and came up with a list of favourites for the sled dog derby. Bart Bummer, with his new dogs, tops the poll. Whitey Carson is the second choice. And Busher LeBrun is third. A couple of local drivers are listed third and fourth and we're thrown in among the longshots."

"That's all right," Max said cheerfully, pouring himself some tea and joining his uncle at the table. "Upsets happen in every sport. We may surprise a few people on Saturday. With Big Fella as our lead dog, anything can happen."

Just then Marty came in, his eyes bright, his cheeks flushed. He was grinning from ear to ear.

"Got Melissa home all right?" Max asked.

"Sure did. She doesn't live very far away. It's a short walk."

"You're not getting a crush on her by any chance?"

Marty gave a short laugh. "Of course not. You know me and girls. I've never had time for them."

"Not until now," Max said. "Seems to me my brother's been smitten. What do you think, Uncle Jake?"

"Don't get me involved in this," their uncle said with a laugh. "There comes a time in a young man's life when crushes have been known to happen. Even in an old man's life. But enough about that. You boys have forgotten something haven't you? It's time to feed the dogs. They'll soon be so hungry they'll jump the fence and head for the kitchen."

Max leaped up from his chair and began to throw on his boots. "By gosh, I did forget," he said. "Come on, Marty, let's go to work."

The brothers ran a pail of water from the tap and picked up a couple of boxes of dog food. They hurried outside and went to the dog pen. The dogs bounded over, happy to see them, eager to be fed.

Max opened the gate then stopped short.

"What's the matter?" Marty asked.

"Where's Big Fella?" Max replied, alarm in his voice. "He's not in the pen and he wasn't in the house. Maybe he got out somehow."

Marty whistled and called out, "Big Fella! Here, boy!" He called again and whistled several times. Big Fella always came running when he heard Marty whistle. This time there was no response, no sign of him.

"Marty, go back and look in the house again. I'll check the barn and look around a bit. And bring me back a flashlight." Max tried not to be unduly alarmed but he was really worried about Big Fella's whereabouts.

The boys looked everywhere but there was no

trace of their big husky.

Max was both frightened and almost frantic by now. He said to Marty, "You feed the dogs and give them water. I'm going to look in the woods. See if I can find some tracks."

"Max. It's getting really dark."

"Just give me the flashlight. I'll be back soon."

Max trudged through the snow surrounding the dog pen. There were no tracks. He went to the end of the driveway and walked down the road leading into town, flashing his light into the woods. After walking about two hundred yards, he thought he saw some broken snow in the woods, among a clump of evergreens. He climbed a snowbank and trudged through knee-high snow until he came across some dog sled tracks.

"I'm sure these weren't here yesterday," he murmured, kneeling down to examine the tracks more closely. He followed them for a few yards and then made a discovery. The driver of the sled, whoever he was, had stopped the sled in the deep woods and the dogs had plopped down in the snow to rest. There were footprints in the snow, leading away from the sled and more footprints leading back again. And dog prints too.

Had the driver gone behind some trees to pee? That's unlikely, Max thought. He had all the privacy he needed right where he'd stopped. And why did he unhitch a single dog and take him with him—if that's what he did? Then where did he go? Why did he stop?

Max followed the trail of footprints—they were really deep holes made by heavy boots—through the trees. They twisted and turned until they ended in a surprising place—halfway up Uncle Jake's driveway. Max had missed the holes in the snow when he first started searching for Big Fella.

No wonder, he thought. The driver had broken through the snowbank lining the driveway but had made an effort to cover the holes in the snow made by his boots. He'd filled in the holes with snow and smoothed them over.

Just then Marty came out of the barn and saw Max holding the flashing light. He came bounding down the driveway and said, "What is it? What have you found?"

"Marty, I'm convinced somebody has stolen Big Fella."

Marty was shocked. "My gosh, why would anyone do that?" he said.

"Look at these prints. Somebody tried to smooth them over. And look over the embankment. Those are definitely paw prints although the wind has filled most of them in with snow."

"So what do you think happened?"

"I figure somebody sneaked up here with a dog

team. He stopped in the woods and walked the rest of the way. Must have happened when all of us were in town today. Then he walked right up to the gate, bold as a bank robber, and called Big Fella. You know how friendly Big Fella is. And the thief probably had some food to offer him. He lured him out of the pen, put a leash on him and led him back to the sled. Big Fella would have smelled the dogs waiting in the woods and been happy to see them. Heck, the driver may have even put Big Fella in harness. Had him help in his own kidnapping."

Marty was almost speechless. "I can't believe some rotten person would steal our dog. Let's go tell Uncle Jake what you've found."

In the kitchen, Uncle Jake was on the phone, talking to Emily. He said, "Just a moment," and then to the boys, "Any luck?"

Max shook his head. He was on the verge of tears. "No luck. He's gone."

Uncle Jake spoke briefly into the telephone and then hung up.

"Emily and Melissa are coming over. They want to help."

An hour later, they were huddled around the open fireplace, the flickering light casting light and dark shadows on their solemn faces. Emily and Melissa had blankets over their laps. From his rocking chair, Uncle Jake was saying, "This is certainly a blow, losing Big Fella. It's a real mystery where he could have got to. Let's all brainstorm the situation. See if we can't decide on a course of action."

"I've already called Chief Connolly and he said he'd ask around town," Max said. "He wanted to know if Big Fella had run away. I said he'd never run away. I told him he was definitely stolen."

"But why would anyone steal him?" Melissa asked.

"There are a couple of reasons," Max replied. "First of all, he's a very special dog. Beautiful, strong, intelligent. And he's becoming a great sled dog. That makes him very valuable to certain people."

"But if someone stole him and tried to sell him locally as a sled dog, everybody would soon know it," Marty argued. "Even if they kept him for themselves, everybody would know. It doesn't make sense."

"Maybe somebody stole him because they were afraid Big Fella would help your team win the big race on Saturday," Emily suggested.

"I thought of that too, Emily," Uncle Jake said. "But why would anyone bother? We're not even expected to finish in the top five. Nobody in the race is afraid of us."

"Not even Bart Bummer?" Marty asked.

"Nah. Bart's so confident his new dogs will make him a shoo-in to win the race, he can't conceive of anybody else even coming close."

Emily had another thought. "If somebody stole Big Fella to sell him, they'd have to do it far away. That means a long train ride; let's say to Indian River or even farther. Can't go by car because the roads are still unplowed."

"And Chief Connolly said he'd have the station master check everybody boarding any trains." Max added. "What's more, Big Fella is well-known in Indian River. Most popular dog in town."

"Then he's got to be somewhere around here," Melissa said. "But where?"

"I have a thought but I hate to even mention it," Max said.

"What is it, Max?"

"Well, what about revenge? Marty and I made some people really angry today at the bear wrestling. The Bummer brothers especially. And I'm certain some other people in the crowd were angry when Doc Green cancelled the event."

"You mean some...some creep might have stolen Big Fella and done him harm—just to get back at you?" Emily was shocked at the idea.

"It's possible. A nasty possibility but one we should consider."

Everyone seemed to sigh at once. The dancing flames failed to dispel the gloom that was painted on every face and seemed to fill the room.

"It's getting late," Uncle Jake said. "Let's meet again over breakfast. See if Chief Connolly has anything to report. Max, why not take the truck and drive Emily and Melissa home. Who knows? Maybe Big Fella leaped over the fence of the pen and went chasing rabbits. Maybe he'll be scratching at the door before the sun comes up."

Later, lying in his bunk, his eyes staring at the ceiling, Max said to Marty. "Uncle Jake means well, trying to cheer us up like he did. But there's no way Big Fella is going to come scratching at the door tonight."

Marty leaned over the edge of the upper bunk. "You're right, Max." he said, as tears began to roll down his cheeks. "I miss him so much already. I just hope we find him alive."

Marty's words brought a lump to Max's throat. He reached for a handkerchief, couldn't find one, so he sniffed once or twice and then wiped his eyes and nose with his pajama sleeve.

"I do too, Marty," he sighed and then rolled over on his side.

CHAPTER 13

THE SEARCH BEGINS IN EARNEST

On Friday morning over an early breakfast, Uncle Jake, Max, Marty, Melissa and Emily made plans. But first, Uncle Jake, who'd been on the phone since sunup, brought everybody up to date.

"I just talked to Chief Connolly. He says he's scoured the town and asked everybody—even folks having breakfast at the Bo Peep—if they knew anything about Big Fella's disappearance. Nobody has seen him and apparently, nobody knows a thing."

"Did he talk to Bart Bummer?" Marty asked.

"Yes, he did. Went to that shack he lives in first thing this morning. Bart denied having any part in the dognapping—that's what the Chief is calling it. Bart said his sons knew nothing about it, either. Then he made some crack about me and you boys."

"What did he say, Uncle Jake?"

"Well, he told the Chief that if me and you boys

didn't know how to build a proper pen for our dogs, it wasn't anybody's fault but ours. Said we should be more careful in future and not to leave gates open."

Marty exploded. "Why, he's an ass!"

"We all know that Marty. Let's get back to the search for Big Fella, shall we?"

Emily suggested that she and Melissa go door to door, asking questions, starting with Uncle Jake's nearest neighbours. "Maybe, just maybe, somebody found him last night and took him in."

Uncle Jake endorsed the idea. "Can't do any harm. The sooner you get started the better. I'd better stay here by the phone. Chief Connolly said he'd be keeping in touch with me throughout the day."

Max rose from the table. "Marty and I are going to take the dog sled into town. Your other dogs may get a sniff of Big Fella and lead us to him."

Uncle Jake agreed. "Take some food and water with you in case you find him and he's been injured somehow."

In town, Max drove straight to the Bummer shack and Max called out.

"Babe, are you in there?"

The door creaked opened and Boris poked his head out, hair falling into his eyes.

"I want to see Babe, not you." Max stated, ice in his voice.

Babe appeared a moment later and walked a few

steps toward Max and Marty.

"What do you fellows want?" he asked. He was obviously surprised to see them.

"I want you to look me in the eye and tell me you don't know anything about my missing dog and where he might be right now."

Babe hesitated for a moment. He glanced around.

"Look me in the eye, Babe—if you can. Where's my dog?"

Babe mumbled, "Don't know. Haven't seen your dog."

"Is that the truth—the honest truth?"

"Uh, yeah. That's it, the honest truth."

"Okay, Babe. See you in the race tomorrow."

Max wheeled the sled around. With Big Fella missing as lead dog it took a few moments longer than usual.

He and Marty were about to leave when Babe shouted after them, "How you gonna be in the race without your best dog?"

"Oh, I'll get him back," promised Max. "With or without your help."

Babe looked confused. Max could see two of the Bummer brothers standing in the open doorway of the shanty. Another was peeking out a window.

Max yelled, "Hike! Hike!" and the sled dogs leaped into action. He heard Babe call out, "I hope you find him."

Max turned to Marty when they'd travelled a little distance. "Well, what do you think?"

"I think he was lying through his yellow teeth," Marty responded, spitting into a snowbank.

"I do, too," Max said. "But even if he wanted to tell the truth he couldn't very well do it with those thugs he has for brothers listening to every word."

Max guided the sled to the outskirts of town.

"Where we going now?" Marty asked.

"I thought we'd make a big circle around town. If the thief took Big Fella somewhere on a sled we might get lucky and find his trail. And the dogs might get a whiff of Big Fella."

"And they might not," said Marty glumly. "It's not as though they're bloodhounds."

Max was brooding about something.

"What are you thinking?" Marty asked.

"I was just thinking of what Babe said when we were leaving. He said, 'I hope you find him.'"

"So...?"

"Marty, he sounded so sincere."

Marty just grunted.

They drove the sled all around the town of Storm Valley. They saw many tracks from other sleds and assumed drivers had left them in warm-up runs, preparing for the big race, now less than twenty-four hours away.

By mid-morning they were hungry. So they

stopped in at the Bo Peep and ordered grilled cheese sandwiches. Max grimaced but said nothing when Marty poured half a bottle of ketchup on his.

Then Max called Uncle Jake. Chief Connolly had called twice but had nothing to report. Emily and Melissa were still knocking on doors. Their search, so far, had been fruitless.

"Tell Uncle Jake to say hello to Melissa for me when he sees her," Marty said just before Max hung up.

"You rascal. You have got a whopping big crush on Melissa," Max said, chuckling.

"Have not," lied Marty. "Come on, let's go." Marty was still blushing when they paid their bill.

There was one set of tracks Max had seen earlier in the day that had puzzled him. The tracks led out of town and into the bush and he convinced Marty they needed to go back for a second look.

When Max stopped the sled, he got out and said excitedly, "Look, Marty. These tracks go off in an odd direction. They lead to a lot of bumpy ground alongside the railroad tracks. And there are stumps under the snow over there where the railroad men cut down trees. That's a dangerous trail. Why would a real musher take a route like this one?"

"Don't know," Marty said. Suddenly he sat straight up in the basket of the sled. "Max, look at the dogs. They're sniffing the trail. I think they smell the scent of Big Fella. I think we better follow these tracks."

"So do I," Max replied, "This is our last hope." He called out, "Let's go, you huskies. Hike! Hike! Let's find your lead dog."

After the dogs followed the trail for about two miles, Marty turned from where he lay in the basket of the sled and pointed. "We're almost to the place where the train was derailed. There's that big rock that did the damage. It must have taken a dozen men to push it aside. Or maybe it took a big machine."

Max looked around. He sniffed the air. The sky was getting darker and it looked like a winter storm was brewing.

"Where's that hidden place I explored after the accident, Marty? You know, where I found the clues? Remember the cigarette butts and the candy wrapper?"

"Max, it's just ahead and to the left. Right over there on that ridge, behind those trees. And wasn't there some kind of shed nearby?"

"There was. And I remember seeing a frozen pond as well. I'll bet the shed was used as a change room for swimmers in the summer."

He stopped the sled and the dogs flopped to the ground. The Mitchell boys followed the trail on foot and found the frozen pond and the shed. There was a lock on the shed door.

"Listen, Marty," Max said, almost in a whisper.

Suddenly, the door of the shed began to shake as if something inside was determined to break it down. They heard furious barking.

"Hear that!" said Max.

Marty was grinning. "I sure do!"

The shed door rattled once more, then again, as the powerful husky trapped inside all but knocked it off its hinges in his determined bid for freedom. Max and Marty rushed forward.

"Only Big Fella barks like that," Max exclaimed. "We've found him, Marty! We've found him!"

"Hey, Big Fella, hey!" Marty shouted as he followed Max to the cabin on the run. "We're coming, boy, we're coming."

CHAPTER 14
SALVAGING AN ICE SCULPTURE

There was jubilation in Uncle Jake's log home late Friday morning when Max and Marty returned with Big Fella. The sled, with Big Fella in his familiar place as lead dog, came flying through the snow and into the yard.

Emily and Melissa had just returned from their search, after knocking on dozens of doors in town. They were tired and dejected because their quest for news about the missing husky had brought no results. Uncle Jake was equally depressed, for he knew what pain was involved when someone lost something precious. He began to think that Big Fella was gone forever.

He and Emily were working together in the kitchen, preparing a pot of beef stew for lunch while Melissa was working on a salad. Suddenly, Uncle Jake stopped in the middle of peeling potatoes and put down his knife. Outside, he thought he heard dogs barking.

"Emily! Melissa! Come quick! The boys are back!" he shouted. He whirled around and almost knocked over a coat rack and a lamp in his excitement. "And Big Fella is with them, Emily! Can you believe it? The boys have found him."

Melissa and Emily ran to the door and out onto the porch. There were the dogs, running hard, Big Fella in the lead. When Max brought the sled to a halt in the driveway, uncle, aunt and niece ran to greet them—the women in their slippers and Jake still in his stocking feet. They stopped to give Big Fella hugs and kisses and then Emily embraced Max and Melissa threw her arms around Marty.

"This is incredible," Emily exclaimed. "What a wonderful surprise! We can't wait to hear what happened."

"Tell us. Tell us," Melissa urged Marty. "Where did you find him?"

"You all come inside," Uncle Jake suggested. "And bring Big Fella with you. My feet are freezing. Come in and get warm. Then tell us how you found the best dern dog in the North Country."

Sitting at the kitchen table, eating from a bowl filled with hot stew, Max told of the day's adventure in great detail. When he stopped for breath, Marty was quick to jump in with additional facts, a few things that Max had neglected to mention.

"We found him in a deserted cabin in the woods," Max said, speaking quickly, one arm looped around

Big Fella's neck. "Whoever stole him took him there and locked him in."

"Did they hurt him?" Melissa asked, bending to stroke Big Fella's head.

"No, they didn't, thank goodness," Marty said. "But he almost hurt himself trying to break out of that shed. He must have thrown himself against the door a hundred times." He looked down at Big Fella. "You were pretty mad, weren't you, boy? Mad at being trapped in there. Well, I don't blame you." Big Fella whined and flicked his ears, as though he understood every word.

Max picked up the story. "Whoever kidnapped him left him a little water to drink. But when we got there it was frozen over. If they left some food for him I didn't see it. But they may have…"

"Another day in that old shed and I hate to think of what might have happened," Marty said, "He would have been pretty dehydrated. Huskies need lots of water."

Emily prepared a meal for Big Fella and placed it in a bowl. He was ravenous and polished it off in minutes. Then he downed a big bowl of water, his second since his return.

At lunch, the boys cleaned their plates of beef stew and Marty pronounced it "the best I've ever eaten—even better than Mom's."

"When we get home, I'm going to tell her you said

that," Max announced, reaching for the final piece of sourdough bread and giving half to his brother.

Uncle Jake jumped up and began clearing the table. Emily took him by the shoulders.

"You go sit in your rocking chair and relax," she said, "and stay out of the kitchen or I'll tell Doctor Green on you. I'll wash the dishes tonight."

Uncle Jake went to sit in front of the fire, Big Fella at his feet. When the others gathered around him, he said, "We still don't know the answer to a pair of mysteries, do we?" he said, staring into the flames. "Who stole Big Fella and why they took him? Who caused the train wreck? I hope we find out before Max and Marty return to Indian River on Sunday." He started to chuckle. "I'll say one thing. There's never a dull moment around here when my nephews come to town.

"Oh, by the way," he added, "I forgot to tell you something. I got some more bad news today. But it's nothing compared to the loss of Big Fella."

Max was concerned and was the first to ask, "What news? What happened, Uncle Jake?"

"Well, Chief Connolly called today to tell me my ice sculpture was vandalized last night. Apparently somebody poured buckets of hot water over it. My big walrus is now a melted walrus. The Chief said he didn't even recognize it. Looked more like a muskrat to him—a muskrat sitting in a sea of ice."

"That's awful," Melissa said indignantly. "Your beautiful sculpture. I must say there are some rotten people in this town. Is it too late to do anything about the sculpture?"

"Afraid it is, Melissa. The judging takes place tonight." He sighed and leaned back in the rocker. Then he gave Emily an affectionate look. "I really liked that old walrus with his fancy tusks. Oh, well, there's always next year."

Uncle Jake sat back again and closed his eyes. "Hey, don't go to sleep, Uncle Jake," Max said, rising to his feet. "Are you up for a trip into town?"

"Max, let him sleep. He's tired," Marty interjected. "What do you have in mind, anyway?"

"Well, I was thinking that Uncle Jake is a creative guy, a real artist. And Emily has an eye for art as well. I thought they might want to look at what's left of the walrus. If they worked together on it, they might be able to salvage something. Or even make it into something else."

"You mean, turn the melted walrus into some other animal?" Melissa asked. "That's a great idea. Why don't we all go into town?"

Marty was already searching for his parka. "Just what I wanted to hear. Let's all go," he said. "Everybody ready? After we check out the sculpture, we can go to the Bo Peep for an ice cream sundae. I'm treating because I won ten dollars in the fishing derby and I can't wait to spend it."

In town, Uncle Jake circled the ruins of his walrus several times, pondering. The others could see he was deep in thought. Emily held onto his arm whenever he moved because the base of the sculpture was now a frozen sheet of smooth ice. Her first priority was taking good care of Uncle Jake.

He laughed and said, "You know, Chief Connolly was right. What's left looks more like a muskrat than a walrus."

Emily had a thought. "Jake, if you chiselled here and chiselled over there, and if you added two large front teeth it might look like a beaver."

"That's right. Nothing wrong with a beaver. And if I chiselled around the base it would look like a beaver coming up through a hole in the ice, wondering when spring is coming."

"Or it could be an otter," Melissa suggested.

Suddenly Max could see it through his uncle's eye. "The hot water they poured over the walrus made everything sleek and smooth. A little work and it would look just like a beaver's skin."

"An otter's skin is even smoother," Melissa said.

"If you decided on a beaver, it would be easy to add a flat beaver tail if you wanted him out of his hole and crouching on the ice," Emily suggested.

They all looked at Uncle Jake. He'd heard enough suggestions. It was up to him to decide what to do.

"Why don't you young folks run on over to the Bo Peep and have your ice cream sundaes," Uncle Jake said, warming to the challenge ahead. "Emily and I will chisel away at this thing for a few minutes. There may be something we can do to make it presentable. But I doubt we'll win any prize money. Anyway, you can see I've come prepared."

He pulled a couple of chisels and a small hammer from a big pocket in his jacket. He turned to Emily. "There's a broom in the back of the truck. If you wouldn't mind sweeping the loose ice and snow from around the base of the sculpture we may have ourselves a beaver pond, after all."

"That's the spirit, Uncle Jake," said Marty, patting him on the shoulder. "Now we'll leave you two artistes to figure it out," Marty took Melissa by the hand. "We'll see you later at the Bo Peep."

CHAPTER 15

THE JUDGES DECIDE

On Friday afternoon, after Max had taken the dogs for a training run, he found his Uncle Jake at the kitchen table.

"Back so soon?" Max asked. "Your ice sculpture ready for judging?"

"Emily and I fixed it as best we could," Uncle Jake said. "It'll do."

Max said cheerfully, "Big Fella's so happy to be back he can't stop wagging his tail. And I could hardly hold him back on the trail today. Win or lose tomorrow, Uncle Jake, I feel like a musher now. I've discovered the real joy that comes from your sport."

Uncle Jake laughed. "It's great fun, isn't it, lad? There's no feeling like it. Someday I predict they'll have races that cover up to one thousand miles, with thousands of dollars in prize money going to the winners."

"Uncle Jake, do you know how sled dog racing started?"

"Well, I believe it began with the Alaskan Gold Rush. That would be back in 1896. Thousands of people rushed to Alaska and the Yukon seeking gold. And they quickly discovered that getting from one place to another was best done by dogsled. You know how some men are—they like to brag. One probably said, 'My dogs are faster than your dogs.' And another man would say, 'Oh, yeah. You'll have to prove it. Let's have a race.' And pretty soon everybody was racing his dogs. And betting big money on the outcome.

"But even before that, some smart musher invented the sled and the gangline—the line that runs from the sled to the lead dog—or dogs because sometimes there are two lead dogs. Each dog is connected to the gangline with a short tugline. Then there's a neckline, which is attached to the dog's collar and keeps him close to the gangline. You're probably familiar with those names by now."

"Well, yes," said Max. "But I still have some questions. For example, is the lead dog always a male?"

"No, the lead dogs are chosen because they are natural leaders and very intelligent. They can be male or female. Two point dogs come next. They are usually the fastest dogs. Then come the swing dogs. Their main job is to turn the sled in the direction taken by the lead dog. The dogs closest to the sled are the wheel dogs. They may take up the rear but they're very important because they pull the most weight. So they have to be strong dogs."

Max had been counting. "That's seven dogs or eight if you count two lead dogs."

"Unfortunately, we don't have another lead dog in Big Fella's class. He'll just have to do it on his own."

Max was a little worried about having one less dog than the maximum allowed for the race. "So we've got seven dogs. And all of the other teams will have eight."

"Don't worry about it. One dog won't make that much difference," Uncle Jake assured him. "You'll be just fine. Nobody expects you to win because you're so young. You're a rookie. But I've been watching. And I know you've quickly become an excellent musher."

Max sighed. He was a little nervous about competing in the big race. But talking to Uncle Jake always made him feel better.

"Oh, by the way," Uncle Jake said, "Doc Green stopped by while you were gone. He's really pleased with my progress and says I should be able to return to dog racing next season. And another thing, your parents called."

"They did? Is there anything wrong at home?"

"Not at all," said Uncle Jake. "They called to say they're coming up on the evening train. They want to be here tomorrow to cheer you on in the race. And they want to make sure I'm as healthy as I told them I was. You and Marty will be going back to Indian River with them on the Sunday train. I'm sure going to miss you boys."

"We'll miss you too, Uncle Jake. But you'll have Emily to come around and keep an eye on you." Max kidded his uncle, "I see you've been keeping an eye on her as well."

Uncle Jake chuckled. "Both eyes, lad. She's certainly brightened things up around this place, hasn't she? And her niece, Melissa, seems to have found a good friend in Marty."

"I've never seen Marty in such a state. Looks like puppy love to me," Max said. "I went through it when we lived in Haileybury. I imagine he'll get over it."

"Don't be too sure, Max. I met Emily when she was about Melissa's age and fell hard. I still feel the same way about her today."

"I've still got a lot to learn about this love and romance business," Max replied. "But I'm glad for Marty. It's good that he has someone other than me to be with. By the way, where is he today?"

"He's with Melissa, of course. They went tobogganing. Then they're coming back here to get you. They want you to go into town with them and be there for the judging of the ice sculpture."

"Hey, great," Max replied. "Are you coming too?"

"No. Emily and I are going to meet for afternoon tea and have a little chat." His eyes twinkled. "We have some issues we have to discuss. And I'm not optimistic about my chances of winning the ice sculpture contest, anyway. You can tell me the results later. There's no rush."

Moments later, Marty and Melissa showed up, their faces flushed from the tobogganing. Or from just being together, Max thought.

"Let's go, brother," Marty said. "We want to be there when they award Uncle Jake first prize money. I'll claim the prize money for you when you win it, Uncle Jake. If Max gets hold of it, he'll want to spend most of it at the Bo Peep."

Max laughed and said, "Uncle Jake knows who has the sweet tooth in this family. And who's making the Bo Peep a regular stop. We'd better let Melissa hold the prize money."

The three teenagers arrived in town just in time to join the crowd waiting to hear the judges' decision. Doc Green's wife was head of the judging committee and she made the announcement in the town hall.

"Ladies and gentlemen, again this year we are fortunate to have half a dozen lovely ice sculptures enhancing our Carnival," she began. She explained that the judges had had a very difficult time deciding on a winner. They had been particularly impressed with Jake Mitchell's sculpture because he took a damaged piece of art—a walrus vandalized by persons still unknown—and brought it back to life as a beaver. It had turned out to be a lovely work of art. "Well done, Jake," she said. She looked over the faces in the crowd. "Is Jake not here today?"

"No ma'am," Marty called out. "But I'll take his prize money to him."

Mrs. Green put a gloved hand to her mouth and blushed with embarrassment.

"Oh, I'm so sorry. I didn't mean to imply that Jake was the winner of the contest," she said, looking directly at Marty. "I'm sorry if I left that impression. No, the winning ice sculpture for this year's Carnival, for his excellent depiction of a bear with her cubs is—Babe Bummer. Congratulations, Mr. Bummer."

A buzz of surprised murmuring swept through the hall. Nobody associated the name Bummer with ice sculpture or art of any kind. Getting into mischief was the Bummers' forte. If there were awards for troublemaking, the Bummers would have won them all—hands down.

There was a smattering of polite applause as an equally surprised Babe made his way forward to claim the prize money and a small trophy. He ignored the whispers and puzzled looks and made a brief acceptance speech. "Thanks, Mrs. Green. This is the first time I ever won anything and I do appreciate it. Thank you."

Later, outside the hall, Marty grabbed Max by the elbow. Marty was indignant. "How could anyone beat out Uncle Jake at sculpturing? Especially Babe. Have you seen his sculpture? Last year the Bummers embarrassed themselves with a goofy sculpture of a sled dog pooping in the snow. They thought it was a hoot. I'll bet Babe's sculpture this year isn't much better."

"But Babe didn't sculpt last year's bombshell, his brothers did," Max pointed out. "And no, I haven't seen his winning entry. It was covered over with a sheet when we passed it last night. So let's go look at it."

They marched down the street and stood in front of Babe's winning sculpture.

There, carved in ice, was a mother bear standing next to her two cubs.

It was Melissa who broke the awkward silence.

"Those cubs are adorable," she said, moving closer. "And the mother bear is perfectly proportioned."

Max and Marty stood there, staring at Babe's depiction.

"Well, it's not bad," Marty said, grudgingly giving credit.

"Be fair, Marty," his brother responded. "It's just about the best dern ice sculpture we've ever seen.

Who'd have believed it?"

"Maybe Babe sneaked a professional into town late at night and paid him to do this." Marty suggested. "People around here say a Bummer will do anything to win."

"Not this time," Max replied. "Come on, Marty, give Babe some credit. He's got a real gift for this sort of thing, just like Uncle Jake."

"Do you think your Uncle Jake will be disappointed at not winning?" Melissa asked.

"Certainly not," said Max. "He'll take it in stride. He knows his walrus was better than his beaver. But even his walrus might not have been good enough to win out over Babe's three bears. He'd be the first to congratulate Babe. Nobody's a better sport than Uncle Jake."

CHAPTER 16

THE BIG RACE BEGINS

It was Saturday morning. Swirling winds and a leaden sky greeted the mushers when they gathered at the lake. Another big crowd was there to see the sled drivers off. When they returned hours later, one of them would be five hundred dollars richer. The voice of the starter bellowed through the megaphone held tight to his mouth. "Number One! Number One to the starting line."

Bart Bummer said, "That's me, boys. I'll be first away and the first one back." He turned to the starter and bragged, "You're looking at the best team and the smartest driver. So be sure and have my prize money ready when I get back."

The starter gave Bart a sour look, and then raised his arm.

Bang! The starter's gun went off and a roar went up from the crowd as Bart Bummer's sled raced away across the trail that initially followed the shoreline of the lake. Within seconds Bart Bummer's sled had disappeared among the evergreens.

"Number Two! Number Two to the line."

The second sled to depart was Bart Bummer's second team—all good dogs—with Babe Bummer, the musher. A minute passed—the interval agreed upon to avoid congestion on the trail.

Bang!

"Hike! Hike! Hike!" shouted Babe as he took off in pursuit of his father's team. As he sped away, Babe looked over to where Max was positioned. He appeared startled when he first saw Big Fella in the harness, anxious to tackle the trail. Then he did something that surprised Max. He smiled. Not meanly. But one of genuine relief. Whitey Carson, looking fit and confident, took his place at the start line. At the gun his powerful team raced away to a round of applause. Whitey waved to the crowd, showing his appreciation.

A similar send-off was given Busher Lebrun, the widely respected French Canadian veteran.

Both men had won important races from New Hampshire to Alaska. It was considered a great honour to have them enter teams in the Storm Valley event. Six more mushers, all local men, took their dogs and sleds to the line and one by one they took up the chase.

Finally, it was Max's turn. He would be the last to

leave. Bart Bummer had already been on the trail for almost nine minutes.

Bang!

"Hike, Big Fella, Hike!" The powerful lead dog yipped twice and lunged forward. The harness tightened as the other dogs, reacting to their leader, leaped into action.

The sky was black in the north and a rising northwest wind swept swirls of snow across the trail, throwing granules in the air that were as hard and fine as desert sand. "Ouch!" Max yelped, as several stung his exposed cheeks.

The course began with an easy eight mile run along the shore. Then it veered left across the lake for about seven miles, followed by another swinging left-hand turn into the woods on the far shore. It ran through the trees on the sloped hills down to the far end of the lake, a twisting nine-mile run through thick growth, gullies and ravines.

At the end of that stretch, each of the mushers would check in with Ron Jackson, a race official who had taken over a deserted cabin once used by prospectors. All drivers would rest at the cabin for a minimum of ten minutes, enough time for the mushers to feed and water their dogs and catch a bite to eat themselves.

The mushers had been assured that Jackson would have a fire blazing in the potbellied stove and a huge pot of bean and bacon soup waiting for the hungry drivers.

The mushers would eat but not linger. They would provide for their dogs and then get right back on the trail. They'd tackle the dash back across the lake, a gruelling run of some twelve miles with another checkpoint at the end of it. There'd be another small cabin on the shoreline, with more food and water and warmth. And another outhouse. After a second ten-minute rest, they'd turn again, this time heading for home, battling the full brunt of the wind and snow for the last ten miles of the race.

The winner would be the musher with the fastest time, not necessarily the first musher to reach the finish line.

The first prize money was five hundred dollars—two hundred and fifty dollars for second place and one hundred dollars for third.

Max jogged along behind his sled at a good, steady pace. He knew there would be dirty weather ahead and he didn't want his team to waste precious energy at the beginning of the event. Their character and determination would be well tested before the day was over.

The obstacles ahead included every kind of terrain: hills and valleys, springs and small streams, rocky outcrops and scrub timber. You could wreck your sled and break your leg if you slid into a tree or bounced off a hidden rock. You could lose your way out on the lake if a storm blew up and blotted out the trail. Max was new to this sport—a rookie. He wanted to travel fast but he knew he must be careful.

He hadn't gone far when he passed two of the local mushers. One had tried to pass the other and failed. The sleds had collided and gone off the trail. The dogs were all tangled up and the mushers were arguing heatedly, each blaming the other. They hardly looked up as Max raced by.

At the end of the first leg, just before he turned out onto the lake, he came across another local driver in trouble. The musher had misjudged the turn and his sled had skidded off a rise into a gully below. The man was working feverishly trying to get things straightened out and get back in the race. Max figured he'd never make it and if he did he'd be closer to last place than first.

"You're doing well, Big Fella, doing well," Max howled into the wind. And he let Big Fella pick up the pace as the sled moved at a much greater speed after it crunched into the hard-packed snow that covered the lake. No longer fearful of hidden rocks or the stumps of trees, Max became bolder. He passed one musher, then another. His dogs were still eager to run, while theirs were already beginning to tire.

Max himself was still fresh and optimistic. He was too new to the sport to know whether or not he should feel a lot of pressure or stress. He knew he was enjoying the excitement of the race, which brought into play the forces of nature, the skill of the musher and the speed and stamina of the well-trained dogs. He was young and tough as whipcord.

His stomach was flat as a floorboard and strong muscles in his back, shoulders and arms rippled whenever he felt the stress of a sharp turn or the need to push up a steep grade. So far, running behind the sled, riding it down the slopes, guiding it over the hills and onto the lake had been more of a thrill than a daunting challenge. He was beginning to think of himself as a musher, not just a green-as-grass substitute driver for his Uncle Jake.

Race officials had cut down a number of small evergreens and planted them in the snow bordering the trail across the lake. The trees were planted every two hundred yards and served as markers, a signal to the mushers that they were exactly where they should be. *Now that's a great idea*, thought Max. A strong wind sweeping across the flat surface, whipping snow into the marks left by the preceding racers could make the lake crossing perilous. He just hoped the wind wouldn't blow the small evergreens away.

"Follow the markers!" he shouted at Big Fella. "We wouldn't want to get lost out here."

He finished the run across the lake in a welter of blinding snow, whipped up by a wind that howled across the white wilderness that seemed to surround him. He could barely see ten yards ahead of the bundle of energy that was Big Fella.

The sled lurched up a rise and the lake was now behind him. Max figured he'd been on the trail for a couple of hours. The wind was sweeping around to the east and was partially at his back. Driving through the thick woods, the granules of snow no longer cut into his exposed cheeks. He crossed an open stretch and thought he saw something looming up ahead. It appeared to be big and brown and moving slowly along the trail. Could it be LeBrun and his team, slowed to a crawl for some reason?

No, he decided, *it wasn't LeBrun.* It was something else, something much bigger than LeBrun, something very ominous that stood directly in his way.

He braked the sled. "Haw, Big Fella. Haw!" There was a clamour of barking as Big Fella and the dogs skidded to a stop. Ahead of them, blocking the trail that led back into the woods, was a huge moose. Max had been warned to watch for moose on this side of the lake. Uncle Jake had told him to avoid the animals if possible. Even so, he hadn't expected to come across one right in his path. And this particular moose appeared to be more upset about the confrontation than Max was.

The big animal's mean eyes glared at Max and his dogs. It had been burrowing in the snow for buried grass and small branches and had found some.

Stubbornly, it held its ground, spittle dripping from its open mouth.

"We're not going to eat your grass," Max shouted in frustration. "Now get out of our way." The huge animal pawed the snow and Max thought it might charge, like a bull seeing red. It was without antlers. Max recalled reading that moose lost their antlers in the winter and grew new ones in the spring—but it still looked dangerous. And Big Fella was making it angry. The lead dog barked at the moose fearlessly and lunged forward, held back by the harness. It was as if Big Fella was saying, "You don't frighten me, you big brute. Now get out of the way or I'll bite your leg off."

The moose snorted and tossed its massive head. "Oh, yeah? Well, you don't scare me either, you little pipsqueak," might have been his answer in animal talk. Then Max recalled Uncle Jake telling him that an angry moose had killed more than one sled dog.

"Easy," said Max to Big Fella.

Dog and moose glared at each other for several seconds. Max had no weapons in the basket. If he'd had a hockey stick in his hands, he might have whacked the moose on the rump and forced it to back down. He didn't even have a puck to throw at it.

Suddenly, the standoff was over. The moose decided that Big Fella meant business. Small as he was, those teeth he bared sent a shiver through the huge body of the moose. His instincts told him he was up against a formidable foe.

He snorted again and then slowly backed up until he brushed against some evergreens. With a final glare at Big Fella, he turned and lumbered through the deep snow into the woods, gone in an instant.

Max may have imagined it but he thought he saw Big Fella smile and smack his lips in satisfaction. "I did imagine it," he said to himself. "Dogs don't do that.

"Hike, team! Let's move," he shouted. "We've lost some valuable time."

For the next couple of hours, Big Fella led the team through the most difficult stretch of the trail—and he did it superbly. He plunged down steep slopes without the slightest hesitation, he avoided snow-covered stumps that bordered the trail and he led his teammates—including Max—through thickets of evergreens and around massive rock formations. And he did it following a trail that was almost obliterated by snow. *The early starters sure had an advantage*, Max found himself thinking. *The trail hadn't been half-buried when they went through. But I'm not complaining. It was simply the luck of the draw.*

Big Fella led them out of the woods and into a man-made clearing. At one end of it was a small log cabin, with smoke blowing from a stack in the roof.

A few feet away stood an outhouse. Good thing I don't feel a need to use that today, Max thought. But somebody has, noting the footprints in the snow that led to and from the door.

Ron Jackson had heard the barking dogs and was curious to know who was checking in next. He threw open the door as Max braked to a stop.

"Hurry in, young fellow, soup's on," he called out.

"Dogs come first," Max replied. "If you've got some good clean water, I'll let them drink and then feed them."

When the dogs lapped up the water and were fed, they dropped down in the snow to rest, their thick tails up against their noses to protect them from the frigid temperatures.

What wonderful animals they are, Max thought, *especially my lead dog with his thick silver grey and white coat, his black nose, and his exuberance for what he was bred to do*. Of all the dogs he'd seen, Big Fella had by far the most effortless gait, with a long reach in front and a solid drive from the back. Max gave Big Fella and the rest of his team affectionate hugs and entered the cabin.

"Well, how do I stand?" he asked Ron Jackson, who was hastily ladling soup into a large bowl. Max threw himself on a pine bench and waited, a spoon in his hand.

"You're doing well, son. Extremely well," was the answer. "To be honest, I'm surprised to see you at all.

Bart Bummer's been through, of course, and his son Babe. They said you probably wouldn't show up because you'd have got lost in the woods. They said there was a big moose wandering around back on the trail, one that would scare the wits out of you and make you turn back." He put the hot soup on the table in front of Max. He chuckled. "Oh, I'm sure they were just kidding."

"Sure they were," said Max. "They are great jokers, the Bummers. Very funny guys."

If Ron Jackson noticed the sarcasm he chose to ignore it. "Bart has a big lead over his son Babe. Looks like they'll finish one-two. But you can still pass Whitey Carson and Busher LeBrun—if you're lucky. They're in a virtual tie for third and they left here a few minutes ago. But remember they're top mushers. If you finish fifth or sixth, you should feel real proud of yourself. You've got a lot of time to make up."

Max waved a hand in front of his mouth. The soup had been so hot it had almost burned his tongue. And he couldn't wait for it to cool. He put down his bowl and rushed for the door. "I don't plan to finish fifth or sixth, Mr. Jackson. I plan on finishing first—no matter what the odds. Thanks for the soup. I should have put a little snow in it. Cool it off a bit."

CHAPTER 17

LOST ON THE LAKE

Max and his dogs were back on the trail, the howling wind throwing sheets of snow in front of the sled. The dogs gamely pushed on, Big Fella leading them down a steep hill toward the lake. The mere fact he couldn't see the trail didn't faze Big Fella. He could follow it by sniffing the snow-covered ruts left by the preceding sleds. Riding the runners, Max couldn't do much to help his lead dog. He left it to Big Fella to guide them across the ice. Again, Max was comforted by the small evergreens marking the trail, one every couple of hundred yards, pushed into snowbanks.

After they had passed the third small evergreen, which had loomed up suddenly, Max looked back. The cabin and shoreline had disappeared. Ahead, he could see nothing, nothing but swirling snow, driving in thick gusts from the northwest. He trudged on, urging the dogs with shouts of encouragement.

The icy wind cut through his parka like a knife through butter. He had no idea if he was gaining on another driver or falling hopelessly behind in the race. An hour passed, then another. The little evergreens loomed out of the storm one by one and then fell behind. He found he could calculate almost to the second when the next one would appear.

A time came when no familiar tree appeared. *That's strange*, he said to himself, *perhaps it blew away in the wind*. Big Fella pushed steadily on, but their progress was slow.

Max watched closely for the next evergreen, counting the seconds. He counted to a hundred, then two hundred. No marker appeared.

Big Fella floundered in the deepening snow, lost the trail, then found it again. Max went up ahead to break trail but found it a hopeless task. Big Fella's instincts were far better than his own.

He braked the sled. "Whoa, Big Fella."

He realized the tree markers were no longer in place. It might have been the wind that turned them loose, rolling them helter skelter across the snow-covered ice. But Max knew better.

"Bart Bummer," he muttered, angrily. "He kicked the trees loose. Sent them flying away."

That's why Bummer had raced his dogs at breakneck speed to hold first place! Max realized, *to take advantage of the storm and get to this part of the race well in front.* Bummer was the only man Max knew who was capable of such a murderous trick. Murderous because any driver lost in the blizzard might easily freeze to death. Even with the markers to show the way, it was risky business crossing the lake. Without them, in a storm like this, it was suicidal.

Max hesitated. He could turn around and try to find his way back to shore and to Ron Jackson's cabin. He could find what evergreens remained. That might be the safest thing to do.

But to go ahead...

He found himself trembling. From the cold, yes, but also from anger. Losing the race wasn't the important thing now. He could lose his life! And all because of a cheater, a crooked driver. He could almost hear Bummer telling the race officials, "Boys. I couldn't help it if the wind blew those markers away. The storm was too fierce, the markers not planted deep enough. If that young kid got lost and froze to death, well, it's not my fault..."

Max was filled with renewed determination.

"Hike! Big Fella. Hike!" he roared, lowering his head to the wind and plunging on.

It was not easy. The going was tough and the snow very deep. Big Fella lost the trail, floundered about, then found it again. The sled was moving at a crawl now. Big Fella was hesitant, unsure of his footing, the snow ahead of him hard packed and unbroken. He lost the trail again and stopped. He looked back and whined, as if to say, sorry Max.

"Never mind, boy. It's not your fault," Max shouted.

Just then, borne on the wind, Max heard a long, desolate howl. The howl of a sled dog, close at hand, some distance off to the left. His own dogs set up a howl in return.

The wind let up for a moment and Max saw a huddle of shadows a few yards away. Clinging to his lead line, he left his sled and pushed through the drifts toward them.

He came across an upset sled and a whimpering huddle of white huskies. It looked like Babe Bummer's team. But where was Babe?

It was easy to guess what had happened. Babe had left the trail and, in attempting to regain it, had become separated from his dogs. They were curled up in the snow, waiting for his return. But if he'd been foolish enough to wander away, he might never return.

Max stared down at the snow-covered huskies. The mainland couldn't be far away. Perhaps Babe was already there, having left his dogs in disgust. Or perhaps another driver had found him and picked him up. *Babe's a tough kid. I'm sure he's all right.* If Max hurried, he could still catch up to the leaders and possibly win the race.

But if he went looking for Babe Bummer, who might be lying half frozen in some drift a hundred yards away or wandering helplessly in the blizzard anywhere on the lake, it might take hours to find him. Why should he try to find him, anyway? Max thought. Hadn't Babe called him a worthless so-and-so? Hadn't Babe and his brother tried to beat him up? It wasn't as if they were friends. They weren't. It wasn't as if anyone would ever know he'd even seen Babe's dogs. They wouldn't.

He started back to his sled, deep in thought. Then he stopped and turned back. "Heck, there goes the race," he muttered unhappily, throwing up his arms. He and Babe may not have been friends but they were mushers. Mushers always helped each other out. Whether or not Babe would do the same for him wasn't the issue. He knew the right thing to do was to go back and look for Babe.

Casting about in a circle, holding to the lead line of Babe's dogs, shouting "Babe!" every few seconds, Max slogged through the snow. But his efforts produced no results. Max went back to his own sled, ordered the dogs to stay put, and detached all the rope he had. He returned to Babe's sled and tied the rope to the missing driver's lead line.

The much longer line enabled him to cover a bigger area. At the end of the line he couldn't see the dogs at all. *If the line comes apart at the knot, I could be in big trouble out here*, Max thought. But he kept moving, investigating every drift.

Just as he was about to give up the search, through the swirling white haze he detected a dark splotch in one of the drifts straight ahead. Max plunged toward it, the line pulled taut in his hand. He saw a heavy mitt, the red sleeve of a parka, a brown boot. He saw a sprawled body, half covered by drifting snow. There were scraps of paper sticking from a side pocket—a Hershey Bar wrapper and a pack of Sweet Caps cigarettes.

It was Babe Bummer. He was unconscious, but breathing. Max could see that Babe's face was badly frostbitten. Working quickly, Max tucked the lead line under one foot and held it down. *Lose that line and I might join you, Babe.* He took off his mitts and slapped Babe's cheeks with his bare hands, trying to rouse him. He rubbed snow in Babe's face and pummelled him hard with both hands, trying to pull him back from a fatal slumber.

When Babe's eyelids finally flickered and he groaned, Max hauled him to his feet and made him walk. Babe stumbled forward, like a man drugged.

"Got lost," he mumbled, "Lost the trail. The markers were gone..."

"I know it, Babe. But listen! Stay awake. Keep swinging your arms. Get your circulation going. Your dogs can follow mine into town."

Max settled Babe in the basket of his sled and covered him with a thick blanket. He took the lead line and joined Babe's sled to his. He hurried back to Big Fella who looked at him curiously.

"Find that trail, Big Fella!" he said. "I'm counting on you. A man's life depends on it."

Big Fella nosed around and found the trail again. With Babe's dogs following, Max began the slow push into the teeth of the wind once more.

Big Fella lost the trail again and Max went ahead, hoping his longer legs would find it. But no luck. They'd lost it completely.

Max took a huge gamble. He drove Big Fella on a straight run for the mainland. "You must run straight, Big Fella," he barked. "If you don't we'll be going in circles out here until we drop."

The dark bulk of the mainland loomed up far sooner than Max expected and he let out a whoop of delight. He could see a light shining through the window of a cabin. He let out another whoop and directed Big Fella toward it.

Max said to himself, "I've got to hurry. We're in the home stretch now."

Within minutes, the two sleds pulled up in front of the cabin; the dogs were panting hard.

Two men in the cabin rushed out to greet Max.

"Babe Bummer's in my sled," he explained. "Get him inside. He's frostbitten. I found him unconscious on the lake."

The men reacted quickly. They lifted Babe from the sled and placed him on a cot in the cabin, not far from the roaring fire.

While Max fed and watered his dogs, Babe began to come around. He was sitting at the pine table eating a bowl of beef stew when Max came inside. There was another bowl waiting for Max.

Babe looked up and said, "I'm out of the race. I'm staying here 'til I thaw out."

"That's a good idea," Max replied, giving Babe a gentle pat on the back. "I'm glad you're alive."

Head down, Babe stumbled over his next words, trying to find the proper thing to say. Finally, he blurted out, "Thank you for saving my life." A tear spilled down his cheek. "You didn't have to look for me out there. Especially after how I treated you."

"I know," Max said. "But mushers always look out for each other, don't they? I'm sure you would have done the same for me. Anyway, I'm not one to hold grudges. My folks taught me that." He finished his stew and rose to go.

Babe grabbed him by the wrist. "Wait a sec," he said. "While you were towing my sled across the lake, I did some thinking. I thought how close I came to freezing to death. I thought of my dad and how he threw the trail markers away, almost killing me, his own son. It was a dirty trick." He halted, his eyes welling with tears. "He doesn't care about me or you or anyone else. Only about himself. Well, I'm through with him. I'm through with all his mean tricks, too."

The pack of cigarettes fell out of his pocket. "I'm through with these, too," he said, tossing the pack into the fire.

"Did he tell you to cause the train wreck?" Max asked bluntly.

"How did you know about that?" Babe said, surprised.

Max pulled a Hershey Bar wrapper from his pocket. "I found one of these near the derailment. And some Sweet Cap cigarettes. Like the pack you just tossed away. Your favourite brand, right? And your favourite bar. I found some more when I picked you up on the lake." He put his hand on Babe's shoulder. "I even found one in the cabin by the pond, where the train was derailed. That's where you took my dog Big Fella, isn't it?"

Babe didn't say anything for a while. Then an odd look of relief came over his features. "Brutus and I stole your dog, Max. Dad told us to. Same thing with the train derailment. We felt awful about it afterward." He looked away, shame-faced. "At least, I did. We didn't mean to hurt anybody, didn't mean for the train to run off the tracks. And we were going to set your dog loose right after the race today. We didn't want to hurt Big Fella either. He's a great dog.

"What we did was wrong and stupid. I can see

170

that now." He turned to Max. "Are you going to tell Chief Connolly on us? Do you think we'll go to jail?"

"I don't know," Max said. "Let's talk about it later. Right now, I've got to go. I may still have a chance to win this race." Before he left the cabin, he asked one more question. "Did you destroy my uncle's ice sculpture?"

Babe shook his head. "Boris and Billy did that. Dad was furious when he found out I entered the event after he told me not to. Said he'd bust up mine, too." He shrugged. "I guess they only ruined your uncle's. Too bad, too. I thought that was the best ice sculpture I'd ever seen."

"Well, thanks for owning up. That's something, at least." Max pulled on his heavy gloves, tightened the hood of his parka and shot outside.

The dogs leaped to their feet when they saw him.

"On, Big Fella, on you huskies," Max shouted as the sled moved forward, picking up speed. The dogs were happy to be running again. The sled whipped through the trees, headed for the finish line, headed for home.

CHAPTER 18

TO THE FINISH

Max was hardly conscious of his own fatigue. He had learned first-hand that mushers had to be a hardy breed, able to withstand all kinds of weather and trail conditions. In his very first race, he had encountered the worst kind of weather, plus a conniving driver who was cheating his way to victory. Max shook his head. This was not a game like hockey or baseball, sports with which he was much more familiar.

And yet, on second thought, *there were similarities*. Driving sled dogs through dangerous whiteouts and over hazardous terrain required teamwork and trust—a strong relationship between dogs and driver. A similar kind of teamwork was required to be successful in other sports. *And yet*, thought Max, *there were major differences, too*. He'd never seen a baseball game stopped by an angry moose standing on the base path. And he'd never played in a hockey game where players got lost on the ice and almost froze to death.

But in every sport he'd played, the object was to win. And in this event, he'd give it his best shot—even though his chances of winning now appeared to be almost nil. A race was a race and he was not about to quit before it was over.

His sled shot out of the woods and he was startled to see a group of miners alongside the trail, outside a place called Gold Mine Fifty-Six. They cheered him on and told him that Busher LeBrun and Whitey Carson had just gone through, that he was right on their tails.

"Whitey's lead dog has gone lame," a miner shouted. "And LeBrun's team looks mighty tired."

Cheered by the news, Max urged Big Fella to move faster. They rounded a bend and there, perhaps two hundred yards ahead, was Busher Lebrun. Big Fella yipped and gave chase. Within minutes, he led his team abreast of LeBrun and then he began edging ahead. LeBrun looked over, shrugged and fell back.

Now Max had only Whitey Carson to worry about. He'd already conceded the first prize money of five hundred dollars to the cheater—Bart Bummer. If he could finish second he'd collect two hundred and fifty dollars. He'd be thrilled to win that amount. Even a hundred dollars for third place would be something. Still, if a stubborn old moose hadn't slowed him down and if he hadn't had to stop for Babe, first place might have been his. *Oh, well*, he thought, *even if I fail to win any prize money, I'll be proud to just finish the race. I know Uncle Jake and my folks will be proud of me, too*, he decided. *That will be reward enough.*

Max felt renewed strength flow through his body as he entered the home stretch. His legs rose and fell mechanically. On several long slopes he rode the runners. He saw Big Fella look back, as if to say, "Don't worry about us, boss, we're fresh and we're having a grand old time." The dogs crested a hill and raced down the far slope onto the lake ice. Only a couple of more miles to go—no more hills now but a straight long run to the finish. Big Fella and his mates began to yip with excitement, sensing their long day was almost over.

Max was passing through the settled district now. There were small cabins and a cluster of mine buildings. A number of spectators had come out from Storm Valley and lined the shore of the lake to greet the first comers. Max waved and they waved back. Max let Big Fella out a little. The sled danced over the snow. The storm had passed, the wind had died and it was clear sailing to the finish.

To his surprise, ahead and to the left, Max saw a team of dogs struggling in the lake snow, following a second trail. Carson's team—moving slowly. And much farther ahead of Carson, there was another team Max could barely see, almost at the finish line. It's Bart Bummer's sled, Max thought. Has to be. *I thought he'd be home and dried out by now*, he told himself. *Looks like he's pushed his dogs too hard and they're about to drop. Now I have to rely on my finish time to beat his. But the seconds are slipping away and I've still got a long distance to go.*

On shore, people could hear Max hollering commands to his team. "Let's go after them, Big Fella! Show everybody what a great lead dog you are!"

Big Fella urged his team to give everything they had in the last few hundred yards. Their burst of speed was phenomenal, considering the trials and tribulations they'd been through that day. Max loomed up on Whitey Carson, who looked back in surprise. Whitey howled at his team but they failed to react. They were almost done.

Big Fella and his team flashed by, and then set their sights on the huge crowd waiting at the finish line.

But the mad final dash by Max and Big Fella appeared to be in vain, coming too late. Bart Bummer's sled had crossed the line a few minutes earlier. Bart had danced around with his arms upraised—a victory dance. He thought the roar of the crowd was for him, and he waved and blew kisses to one and all.

But the cheers and applause were for Max and his team—still driving hard across the ice toward the dock. The spectators on the dock and along the shore knew that Max still had a chance, still had some time on his side—although it might be close.

There was an explosion of applause when Max and his team flashed noisily across the line. Their final dash had been spectacular! They finished less than three minutes behind Bart Bummer's sled—and that meant they owned the fastest time of the day. A rookie musher and a great lead dog had won the derby.

Uncle Jake was in the crowd and cheered wildly. "That dumb ox, Bummer. He didn't know that Max was closing fast and finished only a few minutes behind him," he said to Marty.

"Let's go see Max and Big Fella!" suggested Marty.

They rushed to Max, who was breathing hard, dead tired but tending to his dogs. Telling them what a great job they'd done. Telling them how proud he was of them.

Big Fella jumped up and licked his face and then nuzzled his legs, his message clear. "You did a wonderful job, too, Max. It's a pleasure being your lead dog."

Suddenly, Max was lifted off the ground. Uncle Jake, both arms around his waist, hoisted him high in the air. "Boy, that was a thrilling finish! I'm so proud of you!"

His parents pushed their way through the throng, and while his father pumped his hand, his mother hugged him and kissed him on the cheek.

"Oh, Max, I'm so glad we came for the race," she said. "I was bursting to tell the people around me, 'That's my son out there on the lake. He's going to win this event. I just know it.'"

She kissed him again. Now he had lipstick on both cheeks.

Marty, meanwhile, was pounding him on the back. "I'm proud of you, too, Max," he said. Then he turned to the crowd and gestured. "That's my brother, the musher. Didn't he run a great race—for a rookie?"

Everyone laughed and applauded. Two pretty teenage girls asked Max for his autograph and Max hesitated, not quite sure whether the girls meant it or not. Perhaps they were making fun of him. When his father said, "Sign you name, son. Those young ladies are sincere. They think you're mighty special. And you know, they're absolutely right," Max quickly obliged, blushing throughout the exercise.

Just as he finished signing, "Too Tall" Thomas rushed up from behind him and locked him in a friendly bearhug. For a moment, Max thought his ribs would cave in. Whoosh—the breath left his body.

Max broke free and punched "Too Tall" lightly on

the arm. He saw real affection for him in the giant lumberjack's eyes. Max caught his breath and grinned at the group surrounding him. "Gosh, why all the fuss?" he asked.

"I lost so much time because of things that happened during the race. I wasn't even certain I won it."

"But you did win it!" roared Uncle Jake. "What's more, the judges just announced that Bart Bummer's been disqualified for cheating. If he hadn't cheated you'd have beaten him despite his head start. His own son phoned in and squealed on him. Said his dad kept yankin' up the marker trees and heavin' them off the trail. By the way, Babe said he would have frozen to death on the lake if you hadn't stopped and saved him. Is that what happened?"

"Yes, I guess that's true," Max said. "I had a talk with Babe. He said he and his brother caused the train derailment by placing a big rock on the tracks. He seemed very remorseful about it."

"Hmmp!" Uncle Jake muttered. "He should be remorseful. Those Bummer boys will be in real trouble when Chief Connolly finds out what they did."

"Babe said his father put them up to it."

"Well, his old man is in big trouble, too. He'll be barred for life from sled dog racing because he's such a cheater. And Mr. Chips finally got up enough gumption to fire him and all his boys from their jobs at the mill. I'm sure the Chief will want to talk to him about the train wreck. The Bummers are facing some mighty serious criminal charges. They're finished in this town."

"You know what I say," chuckled "Too Tall" Thomas as he pulled a chocolate bar from his pocket and swallowed it in one big gulp. "I say good riddance to bad rubbish."

CHAPTER 19

HOME AGAIN

"Here she comes!"

It was Marty who heard the train coming, long before it chugged around a curve in the tracks and came into view, black smoke belching from its stack.

They were all standing in the station, huddled around the potbellied stove when Marty, who'd been on the platform holding hands with Melissa, rushed in with the news.

"Train's about here. It'll take on water and then head back to Indian River. Station master says we've got about five minutes."

There were other groups waiting to board, some of them showing post Winter Carnival fatigue, and Marty spread the word about the departure time. One man sleeping on a bench under a blanket groaned when Marty approached and tapped him on the shoulder. "Better wake up, mister. Train's coming in."

The man waved him away and pulled the blanket over his head.

Uncle Jake was there with Emily, talking to Max and Marty's parents. The excitement of Saturday's race was still the topic of conversation. The windup dance the previous night came in for some comment as well.

"I didn't know Marty was such a swell dancer," Uncle Jake said to his brother Harry. "The other dancers stood around gawking whenever he and Melissa took the floor."

Harry Mitchell chuckled and said, "They were probably just trying to keep out of his way. What he lacks in grace he makes up for in energy. I'm certain he and Melissa created a brand new way of dancing the Charleston. Luckily, Marty didn't injure anyone, although I imagine he stepped on poor Melissa's feet a few times."

"Did you see the young ladies gathered around Max?" Uncle Jake said. "They all wanted a turn on the dance floor with him. And he was good enough to oblige a few of them—especially the Winter Carnival Queen."

Harry glanced out the window where two teenage girls had wiped off the pane and were staring in, looking for Max. They were too shy to come inside. "Looks like my son has his very own fan club," he observed.

"Your boy's a real musher now," Uncle Jake said to Harry. "If Max wasn't going back to school, he could race that team of ours, with Big Fella as lead dog, all through the North Country. And win some dandy prize money too. Lots of it."

"Now don't plant any ideas in his head," cautioned Harry Mitchell. "School comes first with my boys, although the classroom may seem a little boring after what they've been through this week."

"Big Fella's had quite a week too," Max said, joining the conversation. "He's already asleep in his box, ready for a long ride in the baggage car. Marty and I will bring him back next year, Uncle Jake. If you start racing again before then, you'll have to find a new lead dog."

"I'm a patient man. I can wait for the best—until you bring him back for next year's Carnival."

"I didn't see that pitiful bear and his owner anywhere around," Marty said. "I guess they left town yesterday."

"Yes, they did and they won't be back." The voice was Doc Green's. He had come rushing through the door and hurried over. "Glad I got here in time," he said, "I wanted to say goodbye to you boys. Say, did you hear the news? The snowplow has finally cleared the road for traffic. And get this. The first truck headed out of town this morning was Bart Bummer's old jalopy. It was packed with sleds and dogs and old furniture. His four sons were right behind him in a couple of beat-up cars. Yep, Bart and his boys packed up and left before sunup. Before they had to face the music. A lot of folks in town missed their chance to wish the Bummers a fond farewell."

"So Chief Connolly isn't going to press any charges against them?" Uncle Jake asked.

"Too much trouble chasing them down. But if they'd stayed in Storm Valley he would have."

Max said, "Wait a minute, Dr. Green. You said four of the boys left in a car. There are five brothers. Which one stayed behind?"

"Oh, I forgot to tell you. Babe Bummer showed up at my place this morning; he'd been beaten up. Apparently he had a terrible argument with his dad and his brothers last night. Told them he didn't want to leave Storm Valley. Told them he couldn't take their lying, their cheating and their way of life any longer. Bart told him, 'Fine with me, Babe, get lost then. You squealed on me and I won't forgive you for it. Do whatever you want. You'll never amount to a hill of beans, anyway.' So Babe had the courage to stay."

"Babe did that?" Max said in admiration. "Where is he now?"

"In the front seat of my car, wondering what to do next. He's a pretty dejected young man. He thinks

Chief Connolly will arrest him for helping to place that rock on the train tracks and for stealing Big Fella."

"Will he be arrested? Will he go to jail?"

"The chief doesn't believe he should get off without some form of punishment. He may serve some time. Or the judge may decide his family was more to blame for Babe's conduct than he was and place him in somebody's custody. He may get a suspended sentence and have to do some community work."

Max pulled Uncle Jake aside and had a few quiet words with him. Uncle Jake listened intently, nodding his head from time to time. Then Max asked Marty to go and get Babe. "Tell him I want to talk with him and I don't have much time."

Marty was back a short time later, pulling Babe by the sleeve.

"Listen, Babe," said Max. "We all know you made some mistakes. But you came clean. That took some real guts."

"It must have been very difficult, breaking from your family," said Uncle Jake, "especially if you have nowhere to go and not much money in your wallet."

"I have five dollars in coins," Babe said, jingling the change in his pants pocket. "And the prize money I got for winning the sculpture contest."

"That's something," said Uncle Jake.

Emily interjected. "By the way, we all thought your sculpture was terrific—the best. You have a real artist's touch—just like Jake. But what are you going to do with your life now that you're going to be on your own?"

Babe pursed his lips. "Don't know yet. I'd like to do more sculptures. Here's something I did for you," he said, handing Max a small box. Inside was a handsome wooden depiction of a husky, one that looked amazingly like Big Fella.

"Wow!" Max said. "It's great. Thank you, Babe."

"And I brought this for you, Marty," Babe said. From another bag he took a copy of a Hardy Boys book. "I hope you haven't read it yet."

"*The Shore Road Mystery!*" Marty exclaimed. "No, Babe, I haven't read it yet. Now I have something to read on the train. Thank you, Babe."

"You're welcome," he said shyly. "Uh, Marty. From now on I'm going to try to be more like you and your brother. I really came to admire you two this week. Maybe envy is a better word. The way you two stick together and...and try to do the right thing. It was never that way in our family."

"Listen, Babe," Max said, rushing to get the words out because it was almost time to go. "Uncle Jake and I have been talking. He thinks you have a lot of potential. Well, Uncle Jake said he'd consider taking a chance on you by taking you into his house.

You've got some things in common: a love for the outdoors, fishing and sled racing, all that sculpting talent. It might work well for both of you. If you have to go to trial, Uncle Jake said he'd speak up for you. You know, be a character witness. He'll even offer to be your custodian. Who knows? Uncle Jake might become the best thing ever to happen to you. If he takes you in, you'd have to help him out with the heavy work and take care of his dogs. Maybe help him with a garden in the spring. That sort of thing. What do you say?"

Babe was speechless. Finally, Uncle Jake broke the silence.

"Heck, boy. What do you say?"

"I say that's the best news I ever heard," hollered Babe, grinning from ear to ear. He turned to Jake. "Would you really do that for me, Jake, take a chance on me after all that's happened?"

"You bet I would," said Uncle Jake.

Then Jake frowned and added. "There's just one problem."

Babe's face fell, crestfallen.

"What's that, Uncle Jake?" Max and Marty said in unison.

"Well, I need someone else's permission before I can say yes." He put his arm around Emily. "You all know I've always wanted a family of my own. So I asked Emily to marry me last night and she said yes."

"That's great news!" whooped Max.

"Congratulations!" echoed Marty.

Everybody rushed forward to pump Jake's hand and embrace Emily.

When the excitement died down, Jake said, "So Emily and Melissa will be coming to live with me. There's one small room left in the house. That could be for you, Babe, but Emily has the final say."

Emily promptly stepped forward and took Babe in her arms. "Of course you can live with us, Babe." She gave him a kiss on the cheek. "You'll be the son I always wanted and a handsome big brother for Melissa."

"I'll be the best brother in the world to you, Melissa," Babe promised. "And maybe someday Jake will let me change my name to Mitchell. Bummer is such a..."

"Bummer of a name," Melissa said, giggling, finishing Babe's sentence.

"Right," Babe said laughing.

Max pulled Babe aside for a final word. "Everybody's counting on you, Babe. Don't let them down. And to show you how much faith I have in you, I want you to have this."

Max thrust five hundred dollars in prize money he'd won into Babe's pocket.

Babe protested, saying, "Max, it's too much. I can't take it."

Max insisted. "Take it," he said, "It'll keep you going for awhile."

Babe was overcome with such generosity. He shook hands with Max, saying, "Only if it's a loan. I promise to pay you back someday."

Max put his left hand on Babe's shoulder. "Don't worry about it," he said. "It's only money."

"No, it's more than money. It's trust and faith in me, and well, it's a whole lot more than money. Thank you, Max. I promise I won't let you down."

The station master threw open the door and called out, "Train leaving for Indian River and points beyond. All aboard!"

There was a rush to the door with everybody shouting "Congratulations" to Jake and Emily and "We'll be back for the wedding." People pumped Babe's hand and wished him well. They were so nice to him he began to cry into his sleeve. There were hugs and kisses and backslapping. Cries of "good luck" and "We'll miss you."

One kiss was more affectionate than any of the others. Off in a corner, as far away from the adults as they could get, Marty and Melissa had their heads together. Their kiss was prolonged and tender. When they broke apart, Marty pulled a small box from his pocket, wrapped in tissue paper.

Inside was a replica of a fish—a miniature walleye, about three inches long, mounted on a small piece of board.

On the board Marty had scrawled, *To Melissa: Don't catch anything bigger than this until I come back. Love, Marty.*

Then from another pocket he extracted a post card he'd bought off a rack at the Bo Peep. The card depicted a startled fisherman in a small boat, reeling in a monster catch—a whale-sized fish superimposed on the post card. Marty had scrawled another message on the back of the card. *Melissa: This is the kind of fish I catch all the time in Indian River. Come visit me and bring your tackle. Marty.*

Melissa burst out laughing and said, "Oh, Marty, I love your sense of humour." She gave him a big hug. "I won't even go fishing again unless it's with you."

When the stationmaster bellowed, "All aboard! Final call!" Marty turned and ran. He was the last passenger to board the train, his parents urging him to hurry as it chugged down the line. He managed a brave smile when he mounted the steps, Max pulling him up by the hand. He turned to wave, and Max could see a few tears began to slip down his brother's cheeks.

Melissa waved back and smiled, holding her small fish and post card in the air. Her lips trembled and her eyes welled up. Emily put an arm around Melissa's shoulder. She handed her a small handkerchief. They watched the train follow a curve in the tracks and suddenly it was gone.

Jake threw a big arm around each of them. "Let's go home," he said in a soft voice. "Babe is in the truck. He's going to drive if we can all squeeze in." Jake turned to Melissa. "Winter Carnival may be over but there's plenty of winter left. When you're sad and miss someone in your life, it's a good idea to keep busy. I've been thinking that you might like to sample the joys of sled dog racing. With Babe and me to teach you, you might become the best dern female driver in the North Country. Maybe the best musher in these parts, male or female. And in no time at all."

When he saw a smile cross her lips, he patted her shoulder. He said, "Melissa, there's no reason a woman musher can't be every bit as skilled as a man. What do you say?"

Melissa smiled. "I say that's a great idea, Uncle Jake."

"That's the spirit, young lady," he said, boosting her up into the cab of the truck. "How about we start learning later today? That soon enough for you?"

LOOKING AHEAD

Max and Marty Mitchell grow excited about the history of hockey's most coveted trophy—the Stanley Cup. They are particularly curious about one of the greatest scorers in Stanley Cup history—One-Eyed Frank McGee.

"Wouldn't it be a thrill to go back in time and meet the Great McGee," Max asks Marty.

"Sure, but that's impossible," Marty responds. "He played at the turn of the century—around 1900."

Impossible? Perhaps not. Thanks to their friend Chief Echo, chieftain at the Tumbling Waters Indian Reserve, Max and Marty share an amazing dream. They journey down the River of Time to Ottawa, Ontario, where they meet and live with Frank McGee. They learn first-hand what it was like to be a hockey hero when the Stanley Cup was young.